The Commuter

The
Commuter

PATRICK OSTER

Distributed by
Argo Navis Author Services
www.argonavisdigital.com

Contents

Contents

About the Author

Patrick Oster is an award-winning journalist who has covered the White House, the State Department and the CIA. He has been a foreign correspondent in Latin America and Europe, covering the fall of the Berlin Wall and the creation of the European Union. A lawyer, he is currently the managing editor for legal news for Bloomberg News. He is the author of "The Mexicans: A Personal Portrait of a People." More details about him can be found at www.patrickoster.com.

eBook ISBN:978-0-7867-5598-1

Print ISBN: 978-0-7867-5597-4

Original cover and back-cover art: Patrick Oster. www.patrickoster.com

Chapter 1

Before Barnaby Gilbert gave into what seemed like a harmless whim during that glorious Indian Summer, his life had been pretty damn regular. Almost boring. Then came his run-in with the counterfeiters, the Chinese spies, the bent FBI agent, the teenager with the knife and the dominatrix. But on that fateful Friday just before things began to unravel, all seem normal, even calm.

As usual, Barnaby, a doughy, kind man in his fifties, took the 7:52 to Grand Central from his village on the Hudson River, as he did every weekday morning, holidays excepted. Nothing was amiss when he boarded the semi-express, which got him to Manhattan at about 8:40 a.m., according to the famous four-faced clock in the center of the terminal's turquoise-ceilinged great hall. From there, in a brisk walk that took about 15 minutes, if he timed the lights correctly, Barnaby was at his desk on the second floor of Montgomery & Co., management consultants, by nine, when his day began with a yellow legal pad, his favorite pen and a clipboard in their proper places.

Barnaby, who had a cherubic face and tawny, thin hair, could have had an office on a higher floor, where senior management sat, but stairway access to the second floor from the lobby permitted him to avoid the unpredictability of elevator arrivals and departures. Besides, he spent many days out of the office, helping clients work faster and smarter. Office prestige wasn't that important to him. What was important was his job. His job was his life and, in some ways, his destiny.

When Barnaby was in high school, he saw "Cheaper by the Dozen" on TV — one of those Million-Dollar Movie things — and decided to become a time-and-motion man, which is what he was that early autumn day. The main character of the movie, played by Clifton Webb, was that pioneer of motion study, Frank Bunker Gilbreth, as Barnaby learned when he looked into the matter later. Gilbreth's theories, combined with the time-study work of Frederick Winslow Taylor, were the foundation of the profession Barnaby eventually adopted. Gilbreth, whose name Barnaby found strikingly similar to his own, made his reputation by studying bricklayers. He figured out a way to reduce the motion of laying a brick from 18 steps to 5, and a management legend was born. By the time Clifton Webb played Gilbreth in the 1950 film, Barnaby's hero had been dead a quarter of a century. But Gilbreth's impact on Barnaby was as great as if Sandy Koufax had been his godfather and pitching had been his chosen profession.

Barnaby never showed the professional brilliance of his hero, but his job skills were beyond mere competence. What he lacked in creative genius, he made up for in hard work. To be honest, in studying the trees before him, it sometimes took Barnaby a while to realize he was in a forest. He lived in a bubble created by meticulous planning and was rarely distracted en route even when he ventured to other cities for clients. But once he realized he'd arrived in the woods, he eventually grasped the essence of the problem and was good at solving it. In his personal life, he often had a similar, slow-footed reaction to people, who sometimes confused him on first encounter. Or even the second.

He practiced what he preached and organized his personal life as efficiently as his time and movements at work. His kitchen cabinets were stocked so the ingredients he used most often were closest to his stove, an appliance he found to be the smart choice: gas on top for quick grilling and electric in the oven for precise baking.

When Barnaby's wife Gwyneth was alive, she'd worked in the city, and they took the same train from and to their home, having prepared their lunches the night before while they cooked dinner. On weekends, they made two meals at a time, putting stews or pasta sauce in plastic containers so they'd have an easy time preparing supper after they returned home from work. Just in case the unexpected happened, they had a backup supply of meat loafs and casserole dishes in the freezer with the weight taped on container tops so Barnaby and his wife could use the microwave's turbo-defrost function to best advantage.

They were able to eat within minutes of arriving home on the 5:47. On Fridays, as a treat, Barnaby and his wife got up a little earlier than usual and put the ingredients for a pot roast or other cheap-cut meat dish in a slow-cook electric pot. When they returned home, they found those meals done to perfection, thanks to the appliance's shut-off timer and keep-warm function.

That Friday's meal would be no different except for one thing. Gwyneth would not be there. She'd died two years before. It was a sudden, sorrowful event that Barnaby tried not to linger on when it popped into his head as it often did on Fridays, pushing back like a storm petrel. His lips would usually tighten at the sad memory, but he soldiered on, as Gwyn had told him to do in her last days, her face grimaced in pain under a baseball cap clamped to her hairless head.

Aside from efficient cooking, Barnaby and Gwyn had worked out other systems to keep costs low. They used their dishwasher, washing machine and dryer by only running full loads on energy-saver cycles and by letting lighter-weight clothes dry on a line in the laundry room in winter or, in warmer weather, on taut ropes tied to their Norway maples in the back yard.

Post-Gwyn, Barnaby had deviated a bit from this money-saving philosophy. He kept her clothes in her closet and bureau drawers in their two-bedroom cottage. There were a couple of reasons Barnaby had for not giving her business suits and dresses to the Goodwill and getting a nice tax deduction. For one, holding onto them gave him a chance, when he was really missing her, to open the drawers and inhale the lingering fragrance of Gwyn's body powder and perfume. On the practical side, he figured, if he married again, his new wife might be able to use something in a size six.

When Gwyn found out she had bone cancer, far too late in the illness, she'd told him he should get married again if she died. He told her to do the same if she recovered and he died first, though he hadn't really meant it. Barnaby couldn't imagine another man's hands on her. As it turned out, he was the one who was free to look for a new mate. He knew he wasn't very adept with women, but he was keeping an eye out for another "good catch," which was how his late father had described Gwyn.

Dating was the furthest thing from his mind as Barnaby was checking his work agenda that Friday. He got settled at his desk and began typing up his recommendations on the Babcox account. He'd easily spotted inefficiencies that any nincompoop should have been able to see: eliminate most paper files; do computer repairs at night with contract IT technicians working remotely; put timers on computers to shut them down at closing time and install infrared motion sensors on the overhead lights to keep them off when no one was in the room. Thank god for nincompoops, he joked to himself. Otherwise he'd be out of a job.

Barnaby filed the Babcox report and submitted it electronically to his boss, Ralph Bannister. The system should have assigned him the next job from a queue that all time-and-motion specialists drew from. But it didn't, and when he checked the job queue, he found it was empty. That was abnormal — and inefficient. He looked at the "Time Is Money" sign on the wall behind his computer and decided he should act immediately.

He picked up his brushed aluminum clipboard and pristine legal pad and put a fresh Bic Rollerball in his shirt pocket. The Rollerball was a bit of an extravagance, given its premium price over the standard ballpoint the office issued for free. But Barnaby was almost a 30-year man at Montgomery & Co. His anniversary was the following week. He took a little perk now and then, and Mr. Bannister had never complained about his expense accounts.

Bannister was a vice president. There were only five in the company, outranked only by a senior vice president and J.J. Montgomery himself, whose grandfather had founded the firm more than 100 years before. Bannister's secretary Betsy, who was officially an administrative assistant, sat outside her boss's wood paneled office, whose corridor glass wall made it evident that he was in.

"Betsy, I need to see Mr. Bannister," Barnaby said. "It's rather urgent."

Betsy, who was wearing a white blouse with a bow tied at the neck, gave Barnaby a weak smile. She seemed uncomfortable.

"We were just going to call you."

"Ah, so you noticed, too."

Betsy looked confused.

"The work queue is empty."

Betsy took a long breath.

"Yes," she said, drawing the word out.

Bannister was on the phone. Spotting Barnaby, he put his right index finger up as if to say "Wait a minute." He quickly finished the call, got up from his mahogany desk and walked toward Barnaby to greet him.

"Well, that was quick. Come in, Barnaby. Come in."

Bannister was in shirtsleeves, with burgundy braces over a starched white shirt. His gray pinstriped suit jacket hung over a visitor's chair to the right of his desk. Barnaby sat down in a matching tan leather chair to the left and took out his pen to jot down any instructions. Bannister returned to his desk chair, a leather swivel model, and picked up a stapled set of papers from his desk. He read them for a while.

"I see your thirty-year anniversary is next Friday."

"Exactly. I came here when I was 25."

Bannister nodded as if reflecting.

"Who was in charge of time and motion back then?"

"That would have been Mr. Trotter."

Bannister let out a short laugh.

"We used to call him Piggy or sometimes Mr. Trotterbottom."

Barnaby managed a weak smile.

"He was a little strict," Barnaby said, "But we all learned the job from the bottom up, so to speak," smiling weakly at his unintended word play.

Bannister took a moment to get the joke. Then he guffawed.

"Good one, Barnaby. Not many in your field have a sense of humor. You know, all numbers and such."

"Humor puts the client at ease."

Bannister cleared his throat, and his smile disappeared.

"Quite so," he said.

"Speaking of which, I seem to have run out of clients. The job queue is empty."

Bannister sighed.

"Yes. That's what I wanted to speak to you about. I'm afraid there are no more clients and won't be."

Barnaby look perplexed.

"Mr. Montgomery has decided that the time-and-motion side of the business just isn't worth the effort and rental space any more," Bannister said. "People want MBA types to tell them how to make billions, not pencil pushers who can save them only a few million. And usually less."

Barnaby's eyes widened. Surely there must be some mistake. Perhaps he'd misunderstood Mr. Bannister's words. Bannister was still talking to him, but Barnaby couldn't quite make out what he was saying. Bannister handed over the stapled papers to Barnaby, who took them in a state of confusion.

"That's a severance agreement, Barnaby. Very generous. Two year's pay, starting after your 30th anniversary. You have a week of vacation coming, pro rated for the partial year, so you needn't bother coming in next week. We'll just send you a check, if you'll sign that last page."

Barnaby riffled through the papers. He knew what they said. He'd reviewed many like them in the consultant work he'd done for clients. The message was always the same: Here's a big check. Don't blab about any company secrets, and don't sue us for age discrimination or anything else. Or you'll get nothing.

"Health insurance is on us till you're 65, then you can get the government stuff."

"But what will I do?"

Bannister shrugged.

"Enjoy life. You've got your pension and your 401(k). Your house is paid off, I take it."

"Of course."

"Well, you're a man of means then. Go have some fun. Take a long vacation or take up a hobby. Something different."

Barnaby looked at the papers again and tried to hand them back, unsigned. Bannister, his arms folded, didn't accept them. Barnaby put the papers under the legal pad on his clipboard.

"Maybe I could just stay on as a contract worker."

Bannister shook him head.

"Thought of and rejected, and I don't think there's much call for your expertise out there among our competitors if you're thinking of applying elsewhere. We're one of the last big firms to offer the service, at least in its classic form. All the others are selling their 21st Century methods — software and the like. Solutions, they call it. We're still back in the 1930s."

"Our methods are tried and true. Our clients will tell you that."

Bannister leaned back in his swivel chair, his thumbs tucked under his braces.

"It's out of my hands, Barnaby."

"This is all I've ever known."

"Maybe you can start your own business...with little firms and such. Just don't approach our clients. That's part of the severance agreement."

Barnaby said nothing for a long while, staring blankly at the top page of the agreement. Bannister cleared his throat and suggested Barnaby just retire early.

"This is ahead of my schedule. I'm only 55. I was going to work on my retirement plan when I turned 62. That's not for seven years."

"Move up your plans! Go enjoy life now."

Bannister opened a cigar humidor on his desk and drew out two of his Cuban favorites. He gave one to Barnaby, who held it in his left hand, showing no sign that he planned to light up. Bannister ran the length of his cigar under his nose, inhaling the forbidden fragrance. He finally put it in his shirt pocket, patting the treasure.

"Course I can't smoke one in the office any more, but when I get home, I'm going to enjoy one in your honor."

Bannister began nodding as if thinking about something.

"In many ways, I envy you, Barnaby. Imagine having the time and money to do anything you want. God, what I wouldn't give for that."

Bannister, who liked to call a good plan "a capital idea," nodded some more, looking out his office window.

"It's like that Dr. Seuss book," Bannister said.

"I beg your pardon?"

"You know. 'Oh, The Places You'll Go!' Think of the adventures you'll have. A year from now, I bet you'll have a heck of a story to tell."

Indeed he did.

Chapter 2

Friday evening passed in a blur after Barnaby returned home. He focused on doing his normal things to avoid thinking about what lay ahead. He changed from his blue blazer and gray wool slacks into comfortable wide-wale tan corduroys and a navy, cotton V-neck sweater over his white T-shirt. He put shoe-trees into his broughams and slipped into a sloppy pair of worn boat shoes.

The slow-cooked pot roast seemed particularly top-notch at first taste, but he just picked at it. He ate at his coffee table as he watched a public television news program. His glass of cabernet was half full, Barnaby noticed. Full, he said to himself, nodding. He'd always been an optimist and was determined not to change just because of an unexpected turn of events. Move forward. That's what Gwyn would have wanted.

After the news, the station ran a fund-raising program featuring the singing of Irish divas. By the time the program ended, he'd finished an entire bottle of wine, twice his normal quota. He found himself unusually sleepy for that time of night, perhaps because of the extra alcohol and was tempted to turn in early. He forced himself to clean up his dishes and stored the rest of the roast in a sealable plastic container.

By the time he finished, his bed had become an irresistible lure. Normally he slept in pajamas, but he just stripped off his clothes, leaving them in a pile at the side of his bed. He didn't even bother to brush his teeth. By the time his head hit the pillow, he was slipping from drowsy to comatose. After a few moments, he was completely out and spent the next eight hours in dreamless sleep.

* * *

That Saturday he was up by seven and had finished showering and shaving by 7:30. He used a straightedge razor and lather made from soap with a brush. Disposable razors were safer on the skin, but the difference in costs was in favor of his bone-handled Wilkinson. The occasional nick aside, it was the smart move.

Barnaby splashed some Old Spice on his face. Other aftershaves were more fashionable. But aftershaves, his research had showed, were just alcohol with some fragrance that wore off after the initial job of closing the face's skin pores. Old Spice was another smart move.

On weekends, Barnaby would read the local paper during breakfast, but the delivery person hadn't dropped his copy off that day. As he was pouring cereal into a bowl, he had an idea. He got his laptop and brought it into the kitchen. He clicked on his browser icon, went to the newspaper's website and read the day's stories for no extra charge as he ate. He would tell Tesla. She'd be proud.

Tesla was a neighbor girl who'd been coming over for years. Barnaby had first met her when she'd joined a Girl Scout group that his wife had organized. Barnaby and Gwyn had tried to have children, but it hadn't worked out. Tesla had become sort of an unofficial daughter, partly because her mom, a single parent, worked a late shift at a local hospital and had come to rely on the Gilberts for informal childcare, a task they'd embraced. In middle school, after she'd finished her homework, Tesla would watch television or play with the model train setup in Barnaby's basement. In high school, she'd taken to passing away hours on his computer, surfing or e-mailing friends. A senior at the local high school that year, she'd blossomed into a computer whiz and an attractive young lady, as Barnaby put it.

She'd taught Barnaby all he knew about folders, files and firewalls as well as the pitfalls of e-mail and how to do research on the Internet. Thanks to her, he'd even joined a birding blog. Barnaby's handle was HudsonHawk, which he'd adopted because of his interest in birds along the river that ran behind his property. He hadn't realized there was a rather awful Bruce Willis thriller of the same name. Some of the women on the blog asked him if he looked anything like the movie star or, jokingly, if he'd ever been a cat burglar, like the film character. "Would that it were," Barnaby had replied.

Tesla, was a tall, lanky girl who dressed like a tomboy for most of her adolescence. Barnaby wasn't even sure she owned a dress. She'd taken the SATs and done well. She hadn't heard from all her preferred schools, but Barnaby knew he'd soon have to fend for himself when it came to computers. In the meantime, he hoped Tesla would set up a few things before she left. He had a plan for the future that had come to him over the wine the night before.

By nine, Barnaby was hiking through a nearby point of land that jutted into the Hudson from its east side. A former Native American trading center that had become a 20th Century garbage dump, the area had been turned into a county park that offered swimming, picnicking, overnight camping — and superb bird watching. Optimistic that he would see something new, Barnaby had his 40-power spotter scope and 10-power binoculars in a canvas bag slung across his right shoulder. The unusually warm morning temperature had generated a fog across the far bank of the river, giving the landscape a gauzy Sleepy Hollow look that one might find on a paperback cover of a novel by Washington Irving, whose house sat on a shoreline hill a dozen miles south.

Barnaby spotted the usual denizens of the waters around the point – ducks, geese and hawks – but then got a treat on its south side. A Great Blue Heron, standing in shallow waters at low tide, spread its majestic wings, reminding Barnaby of an icon from a European coat of arms. The bird retracted its wings after its stretch and flew off south, a bit late for its usual migration. Barnaby knew that soon bald eagles, red hawks and other raptors would replace the herons as the weather got colder. They'd come to sit in barren poplars and oaks like salivating diners at a tapas bar, savoring the hairy, scaly or winged offerings nature would put on display.

Barnaby's life list, which he kept in a slim leather-bound journal, was full of listings about gulls, hawks, osprey, egrets, swans and Canada geese as common as vermin. Some were already gone from the point, real-life snowbirds seeking the comfort of the southern sun. The raptors would stay until spring flirted with the region.

Where precisely did the eagles and others go when it warmed up, Barnaby wondered. Somewhere north obviously. Maybe he would follow them some day. Maybe that would be sooner than later, he thought. He suddenly had the time to do it. Take up a hobby, Mr. Bannister had said. He was already a birder. Maybe he would become an eagle tracker. Or even better, maybe he'd do what birders called a Big Year and see how many species he could spot in 12 months across the continent. Within days, he did go on a trek, but he wound up tracking a much more dangerous animal than a bird.

Chapter 3

On Monday, Barnaby awoke at his regular time, fed a mouse to a snake named Herpie and took his usual train to the city. He'd cleaned out his desk at Montgomery & Co. the Friday before. He was officially still an employee of the firm until his termination date, but he had no intention to return to his former office that day. That was the past. His future was to be his own boss. That was the plan he'd worked out. He'd be a consultant to start and maybe form a company of his own with time-and-motion consultants who reported to him. That would show Mr. Bannister a thing or two. People out there still wanted his services. He was sure of it.

He didn't accept Bannister's conclusion that time-and-motion specialists, who people had taken to calling efficiency experts, were outmoded. Time and motion were immutable forces of the universe. As long as profit was the chief motivator of business, someone would want to know how to make money by being more efficient. If Fortune 500 giants didn't want his services, he would offer himself to small and mid-cap companies. Even mom-and-pop firms would make good clients. Maybe they were too small for Montgomery & Co., but Barnaby Gilbert, sole proprietor, would welcome them.

As a good start, the ride to Manhattan cost Barnaby nothing extra that Monday. He had a monthly pass that was valid until the end of November, weekends included. He got a good seat, too. He arrived at the station a few minutes earlier than normal, perhaps because of his excitement about the new world that lay ahead. Knowing where the sliding doors would be when the rush-hour train stopped, Barnaby was first into the car and snagged a spot next to the window on a bench facing forward with the river on his right.

He winked at the conductor, a man named Hank, a no-nonsense ticket taker who had a history of calling local police to yank people off his train if they misbehaved. That usually meant yelling or drinking — but sometimes it was for a lot less. Guff. That was pretty much Hank's threshold for calling the cops.

It wasn't a police matter if people wasted Hank's time by buying tickets on the train instead of at the agent window or the convenient machines at any station, as public service announcements suggested. But Hank showed his irritation nonetheless.

"Gonna cost you a lot more," Hank would say, looking at the poor commuter before saying how much extra it would be. Then he'd collect the premium fare, making it clear that he regarded the purchase as an unwelcome interruption of his morning routine. And cash only. Hank and other conductors had their rules, no exceptions. It was literally their way or the highway.

For regulars, such as Barnaby, Hank grunted a simple "Got it." or just nodded his head as a signal to riders that they could resume reading or chatting with friends — as long as they weren't too loud. For those with monthly passes, which didn't need to be punched or collected, Hank didn't mind if you went to sleep on the way in as long as your ticket was visible in your hand or hanging on a lanyard around your neck. However, if you obscured the part of the ticket that showed the name of your station or whether the ticket was marked for exclusive use of a man or a woman, as all tickets were, Hank would wake you up. He would not be pleased to have to do so, even if he found you weren't using a cheaper ticket from closer-in station or doubling up on a pass issued to your spouse. You would have wasted his time, and he'd say so.

As Hank went through the car after the train left Tarrytown, the last express stop, Barnaby could see many of the regulars: a well-dressed man who wore a Burberry trench coat in autumn and winter, a schoolgirl who got off at 125th Street, an older woman with hennaed hair who often passed Barnaby on her bicycle as he walked to the station, a middle-aged Asian-looking man who read the Times and the Journal, and a garrulous family of four who usually sat at the south end of the car.

Some commuters didn't seem to care about the astonishingly beautiful view the Hudson afforded riders. The Asian man, who got on at Tarrytown, read his newspapers then busied himself with something on his iPad. Others had e-readers and lost themselves in books or Internet news. Those who staked out seats at the extreme ends of the train's cars plugged laptops into provided outlets and watched movies or played games like Angry Birds, which Barnaby found a waste of time, even though it involved bids, a passion of his.

Barnaby was more inclined to look out the window, sometimes pulling out a pair of small binoculars to check out hawks or eagles or swans on the way to or from home. In winter, he'd get a close-up of barges slicing their way north through gray waters and blustery whitecaps, laden with coal or some other burdensome cargo. In summer, he'd check out sailboats scudding up or down or across the Hudson, their parchment-white sails in trim or luffing against waters turned blue by the season's heat and sun.

Barnaby's Internet research had taught him that the Hudson was not actually a river but an estuary whose tides pushed or pulled vessels from New York Harbor to the state capital, creating a brackish waterway in their wakes. Barnaby dreamed about owning a sailboat to ply the Hudson one day. He and his late wife had discussed the matter a few times, but she was not a good sailor, and the idea never got anywhere.

After she passed away, Barnaby had thought about at least getting a small boat, maybe a 14-footer with a drop keel that he could handle by himself. But docking was a tricky matter, his research at the local yacht club had showed him, and he held back on that purchase until he could get himself a partner.

The previous spring, he'd considered drafting Tesla as his first mate. She was probably stronger than he was, thanks to her regimen of running, free weights and yoga. But he never got around to asking her, partly because his weekend birding kept getting in the way. As he thought about that during the ride to work, he conceded that the time had probably passed for his dream. Sailing season was almost over and wouldn't resume till the beginning of May, just a few months before Tesla went off to college.

Before she did, he suddenly realized, they'd have to decide what to do with her reptile and amphibian collection. Her mother, who had a calm demeanor in the face of squirting blood or severed limbs, was squeamish about her daughter's unusual pets and was all too happy that they were being kept at Barnaby's. There was Hortense, a ball python who favored live dining, Herpie, a scarlet kingsnake who preferred to eat dead rodents, Fred, a snapping turtle who seemed to eat anything, and a desert lizard Tesla called Frenchie because he had a very active tongue. The newest zoo members were two bullfrogs in search of names. Jeremiah and Froggy were in the running.

Tesla's interest in herpetology started at the age of four with a small box turtle her late father had bought her. After the turtle mysteriously disappeared, Tesla asked the Gilberts if she could keep a replacement pet at their house. Barnaby's wife agreed, thinking they'd signed up for another little turtle. When it turned out to be a large snake, she was reluctant to go back on her word, and so began Tesla's slimy little zoo.

To Barnaby, snakes were not something one naturally wanted to pet like a dog or a rabbit. But he grew to like them as he learned more about their habits. Hortense, who was about five feet in length, was the first member of Tesla's collection. Barnaby took to her more than he would have imagined after Tesla pointed out that his beloved birds and reptiles had common ancestors and both produced their young with eggs.

Tesla had also introduced him to the world of computers and electronic gadgets. She persuaded him to buy an MP3 player after telling him she could convert his vinyl opera and show tunes LPs to digital files so he could enjoy his music on the go. She tossed in her own entries that sometimes startled Barnaby when he put his device on shuffle mode and found he'd gone from Kurt Weill to Kurt Cobain.

The noisy family that haunted Barnaby's usual car broke his train of thought about Tesla with their cacophony. In his experience, they argued about almost everything. Their angry patter that day was about what to have for dinner. They seemed to relish their otherwise unappealing facing, windowless seats at the end of the car, perhaps because they could bicker almost nose-to-nose to make their loud points. They only bickered when Hank the conductor wasn't in the car, as he wasn't at that moment. The fussy man in the Burberry coat had complained to Hank a couple of times about their noise when he'd gotten stuck with a seat near theirs. After the second time, Hank had threatened to bar the quartet from the train. They'd moved to another car. But they were back in Hank's realm that day, perhaps exiled by some other scratchy ticket taker.

They reminded Barnaby of a family he'd heard on a local station that broadcast programs from the golden age of radio.

The Bickersons. In character, Don Ameche and Frances Langford also argued about everything, big and small. Barnaby never did learn the last name of the family on the train, but for him, they'd become the Bickersons.

He'd given nicknames to most of his train's regulars. The woman with the hennaed hair was Helga. Often dressed in dark suits with expensive leather pumps, she favored harsh makeup that gave her a bossy Germanic look. Barnaby imagined that she ran a high-end antique shop in the city. Based on her tailored clothes, she made a good living, whatever it was. But her bike rides to the station showed she had a frugal side that he found intriguing. More than occasionally he caught himself staring at her.

The Asian-looking gentleman, who usually sat by the window on the non-river side of the car, was Jackie. In the morning, he would occasionally make short cell-phone calls. Barnaby could not make out what he said. The man wore designer casual clothes year-round and spoke in a foreign language. Barnaby guessed it was Chinese. He was hopeless when it came to languages other than being able to point to phrases in travel guides to get what he needed in restaurants or hotels when he and his wife had traveled.

The man might be Korean or from Southeast Asia for all Barnaby knew. Barnaby would never say it publicly, but Asians all looked alike to him. It was nothing racist as far as he knew. He was just ignorant and willing to admit it. Not sure if the man was Chinese or Chinese-American or even Chinese Canadian, Barnaby called him Jackie because he looked a bit like a tall Jackie Chan, the martial-arts actor.

Ignorance, cultural or otherwise, was not necessarily a bad thing in Barnaby's experience. You just needed to deal with it, as he usually did on a job. Ignorance plus lack of curiosity was a deadly combination, but curing ignorance with questions was the beginning of wisdom, Barnaby had read once in a book, and he believed it to be true. On the job, he asked the most basic questions of clients to get himself situated. Often the answers proved revealing both to him and his customers.

As he reflected that Monday on what he'd learned about all his fellow passengers in his years of commuting, he found he didn't really know much. He had a hmmm- moment about that unexplored frontier. And so an idea began — only to be interrupted by the Hank's penetrating voice over the train's balky intercom. He was barking out an announcement that 125th Street would be the next stop and Grand Central, the end of the line, was after that.

The henna-haired woman, who sometimes went all the way to Grand Central, got off at 125th. So did the schoolgirl, dressed in a powder-blue pleated skirt and round-collared light blue blouse. She stood and zipped up her black sleeveless fleece, which set off her white, spiky hair. She reached back to her seat and slung a red canvas knapsack over her right shoulder.

In front of her in line were some adult passengers, mostly Hispanic and black, and some other kids who looked like students. Barnaby guessed the schoolgirl wouldn't be getting off for some destination in Harlem but would change for the subway to get to wherever she was going south or west. Probably the northern part of the Upper East Side.

Harlem was an unlikely place for a young white girl to be walking around even in daylight hours. Or was it? Barnaby himself had never been to Harlem. He'd read about its renaissance, especially after President Clinton had opened an office there after his second term. Maybe he would get off the train one day with her to find out what it was like – and maybe where she went. Or follow Helga. That unexplored frontier. But not that day. He had a different plan for that day.

Once in the city, he wanted to see what it would cost to rent an office, maybe one near Montgomery & Co. The office would be a base for the new time-and-motion business he planned to start. He had no appointments with real estate agents. He just planned to walk about and scout locations. And then it came to him. Realizing his time options were flexible, he decided he might be able to multi-task. The office hunt and the new frontier. As he reconnoitered the office situation, he might be able to follow one of his fellow passengers who got off at the end of the line to see where he or she went. The person might even work in a building that would be suitable for Barnaby's new office. That would be efficient!

In fact, he could pick a different person every day and see where he was led. It would be a bit like birding. And, as he did with his winged subjects in their habitat, he could record his findings of the human species in a journal and maybe even take pictures. A life list of the most interesting species of all. Nothing invasive, or course. He wouldn't bother people or even talk to them if he could avoid it. Just observe. It could become that new hobby Mr. Bannister had suggested. Barnaby smiled at his inspiration. As Mr. Bannister might say, it was a capital idea.

But which one to follow first? As Barnaby was considering the answer, he noticed he was in line right behind Jackie as the train was emptying out. Once inside Grand Central, which he'd learned from Hank was a terminal not a station, Barnaby followed Jackie as he headed south. The Asian-looking man walked the same path that led to Barnaby's former office. In times past, he'd noticed the man striding before him, but Barnaby had always broken off from him to go to work, wondering where he went and what he did for a living. Now perhaps he would find out.

As Barnaby got to his former office, he ignored it for the first time and continued down Park Avenue to see where Jackie would go. At 34th, where Park became Park Avenue South, he could see that the light was red and that Jackie had stopped and was waiting for it to change. Barnaby thought about stopping too to keep his distance. But before he could, the signal turned green, and the man, dressed in a lightweight black leather jacket over a black silk shirt and well-creased charcoal wool trousers, crossed the street, heading south.

Around 25th Street, the man turned west into an area that was an unofficial mall for wholesale shops offering Korean furniture, designer watches and brand-name perfume. In the middle of one block, the man entered a building that had only a number on the glass front door. Barnaby considered going in immediately to see which floor the man was headed for. But that would put him right on top of the man and perhaps in the same elevator with no real explanation for why he was there. The man might even recognize him from the train, and then what? His new hobby was proving more of a challenge than he'd expected, but he found it strangely exciting. Like being on a big-game hunt.

He decided to walk to the end of the block to think things out, turning his head occasionally to keep an eye on Jackie's building. Maybe, he thought, he could go in the building and ask if they had an office for rent. Or he could follow Jackie another day. As with birding, Barnaby realized he needed to be patient and learn his quarry's habitat.

He'd brought along some pens, a clipboard, a legal pad and a point-and-shoot camera in a tote bag, which he'd gotten as a premium for contributing to his local public radio station. He'd packed the supplies to help him search for a new office, but he realized the same things might be useful for his new hobby. He could make notes on his subjects and maybe snap a photo.

Barnaby had been lucky in dressing more casually that morning than he would have for a normal workday. He'd chosen a navy poplin zip-up jacket, a blue buttoned-down broadcloth shirt, cotton khaki pants and sensible Clarks walking shoes. He didn't look like anyone important or threatening. He blended in. Perfect for tracking.

He decided he needed a cover story if Jackie or anyone confronted him about what he was doing. One yarn he came up with was that he was just a tourist, poking around the city — hence the camera. Or, with a list of questions typed out, he could be a survey taker. He loved the idea of having a clipboard and a questionnaire. You could do anything with a clipboard. He could be someone seeking signatures for a petition. Clean up the Hudson, more public bathrooms in Manhattan, that kind of thing — but nothing controversial like abortion or gay rights. He was in the midst of making this mental cover-story list when he noticed he'd arrived at the street's corner. He stopped and pivoted so he could look back at any activity in front of Jackie's building. Nothing.

"Need some cologne?" another Asian-looking man asked out of the blue. He was standing in the entrance of a perfume store Barnaby had just passed. "Good price."

Barnaby turned toward the man, glanced back at Jackie's building again, and, seeing no activity, moved closer to the store to examine the wares in its window. He smiled as he realized the man had given him a valid reason to be in the neighborhood. Shopping. But then he noticed a store sign that read: "Wholesale Only." Below that warning were short messages in what appeared to be Spanish and ideographs in Chinese or perhaps Korean. Barnaby wasn't sure.

"I'm not a wholesaler," Barnaby replied, sounding discouraged.

The man looked left and right, then said, "You got cash?"

Barnaby did. He usually carried a couple of hundreds dollars that he withdrew from his bank ATM. His bank charged fees for each ATM usage over a minimum number per month, so paying in cash for groceries or dry cleaning was cheaper in the long run, he'd calculated. It was the smart move.

Barnaby nodded at the man's question. The man extended his right arm to beckon Barnaby into the store. Barnaby realized he wouldn't be able to watch Jackie's building from inside, but he decided to take a chance. He had no real need for men's cologne, but Jackie might be in the wholesale business. He'd use the opportunity to suss out his turf.

Inside, on glass shelves that were backlit and stretched to the ceiling, were thousands of boxes of cologne and aftershave for men and perfume, eau de cologne and powder for women. Barnaby recognized the designer names he'd seen in magazines that offered free samples in aromatic scratch-and-sniff inserts. The man brought several of them down and put them on the glass counter near the cash register.

Barnaby was the only one in the store and wondered, given the early hour, if he might be the first customer of the day. He'd read that store managers considered it good luck to make a sale to the first customer and bad luck if they didn't. He wasn't looking for a bargain, but he was amused at the prospect of a high-pressure pitch.

"Could I have a sniff," Barnaby said.

The man grabbed Barnaby's right arm and sprayed one of the colognes from a jet-black bottle on his right wrist. Startled at first, Barnaby let the cologne dry and smelled it. His nose crinkled.

"A bit strong for me."

A slim Asian-looking woman joined Barnaby and the man, picking up another cologne that looked like thin lemon juice though the clear glass of the bottle.

"This is for the mature man," she said, spraying it on his left wrist, which she held onto. She inhaled the fragrance and made a sound of pleasure without opening her mouth. "The ladies love this one."

Barnaby slipped gently out of her grasp and asked how much it cost. The man gave the price, which made Barnaby's eyes open a bit. The man looked at Barnaby, then said, "You pay twice as much at Bloomingdale's."

"I buy mostly online."

The man paused, then asked: "What kind of cologne do you use now?"

"None really. Just some Old Spice."

The man's eyes and nose pinched together. The woman walked away. From under the counter, the man produced another bottle that looked very similar to the lemony liquid.

"Smell this one. Same thing but cheaper."

Barnaby sniffed the residue of liquid on the sprayer nozzle of the bottle then squirted a bit from the more expensive bottle. His eyebrows raised and his head nodded in approval.

"I can't tell the difference."

"This one ten dollars," the man said, pointing to the cheaper bottle.

"How is that possible?"

"Special deal. This week only."

"Well, if they smell the same but one costs less, who would be able to tell what you paid once it was on your face?"

"Exactly."

Barnaby considered the purchase. He didn't really need the cologne, but it didn't cost much, and it gave him a prop in case he needed to walk around the neighborhood looking like a shopper.

"Can I get it with a bag with your store name on it?"

The man looked confused, then said "Sure."

Barnaby handed over a ten-dollar bill.

"Oh," Barnaby said as he watched the man put the money in his pocket. "What about tax?"

The man smiled.

"No tax today. Tax-free shopping day in New York."

Barnaby, encouraged by his efforts in blending in, retraced his steps to the building Jackie had entered. Armed with his shopping bad, he went into the lobby, which was empty. On the building directory were a list of about a dozen tenants, most of them export-import companies, many with Chinese-sounding names like Shanghai Ex-Im Enterprises.

To the right of the lobby, which had a black-and-white tiled floor, was a door that said "Manager's Office." Barnaby knocked gently, then harder after there was no response. He heard footsteps and a man, not Asian in appearance, opened the door and said, "Yeah?"

"I'm thinking about renting an office and wonder if you have any vacancies."

The man took a long look at Barnaby and said, "Not really."

"Does that mean something might open soon?"

The man paused.

"Maybe."

"How much would the rent be and how big a space is it? I don't need a lot."

The man nodded as he took in the remark.

"What kinda business you in?"

"Time and motion?"

"Beg your pardon?

"I find inefficiencies in the way people do things and explain how they can do their work smarter and faster."

"And people pay you for that?"

"Yes. I save them money."

The man nodded.

"Takes all kinds, I guess, but I don't think you'd like it here."

"Why?"

"You're not Chinese, I take it."

"No."

"All Chinese here."

Barnaby took that in, not sure what to make of the man's remarks.

"Any other buildings in the area that might have a vacancy?"

"Get an agent, pal. You'll just waste your time doing your own search. I know that much. And be prepared to pay a lot. And I mean a lot."

Barnaby nodded.

"You want to do the smart thing?"

"Almost always."

"If you don't have walk-in traffic in your business, work out of your house and get a website. That's the modern way. Gets the office-in-the-home deduction too."

"You sound knowledgeable."

"I got a cousin who does taxes. Up in Yonkers."

The man reached into his back pocket and pulled out his wallet. From it, he extracted a business card. He handed it to Barnaby.

"You call Angelo. He'll fix you up."

Barnaby thanked the man and left the building. He looked at it from the front, then crossed the street to get a better look. Several of the windows had the names of companies on them. All had the blinds or curtains drawn. Barnaby took out his camera and snapped a picture. To be sure, he adjusted the zoom lens and took a tighter one so the letters of the names were more visible.

"Who the hell is that?" Special Agent Zoot Ames asked from his watching post at a coffee shop across the street from the building.

"No clue," said Zoot's new partner, Plummy van der Graf. "Maybe just a tourist."

"That's not exactly the Empire State Building. Why take a picture of that?"

"Hey, don't snap at me about it. You're just pissed because you're stuck on this crappy stakeout."

"Yeah, yeah, yeah. And I suppose you're thrilled to be here."

"Don't get me started."

Zoot, whose father had named him after his favorite jazz musician, was almost six feet tall and had a well-built physique thanks to nightly calisthenics in his basement rec room in Queens. Plummy was a bit taller. She was what Zoot's mother would have called big-boned, like some relative of Julia Child, the famous food-loving chef.

Both were in a bit of FBI exile. Plummy had been on a more prestigious financial-crimes unit, using her accounting degree to some profit before a drunken shouting match with the agent in charge of the New York office had resulted in her transfer to the dungeon of counterfeit-goods duty. Zoot had suffered a similar demotion from the organized crime unit a few years before. But his offense had been something more serious than drinking and shouting.

Zoot was a St. John's law grad who'd had some brief experience in copyright and trademark law in private practice so his transfer made some surface sense, though his new job was a waste of his encyclopedic knowledge of the crime families operating in the New York area.

"I thought we were the only ones staking this place out," Plummy said after watching Barnaby linger in front of the building for a while, snapping a couple of more photographs.

"That is not a stakeout," Zoot said, pointing to Barnaby.

"What makes you say that?"

"If he's surveilling the place, why be so obvious?"

"Maybe that's his M.O. He looks so obvious, so clueless, that no one pays any attention. Like some nitwit tourist. Could be a brilliant move." A pause. "Or maybe he's a pro but figured all the windows are covered, so what's the danger?"

Zoot snorted a laugh.

"If anybody was peeking through one particular window, he's gonna find out what danger really is."

Chapter 4

Barnaby checked the photos on his camera. After he got home, he planned to make a file on his computer for Jackie, not unlike the ones he kept on grackles, red-tailed hawks and other Hudson River birds. In fact, he planned to make a file for each person he observed. Humans were just another species to observe, so recording them shouldn't be that different, he told himself. Birding 2.0.

He knew he wouldn't learn all about his subjects in just one day, if birds were an indication. He'd build up the details and see what sort of picture he got of people, just as he did in noting nesting protocols, times of migrations and diet. Ideally he'd get some photos of his quarries, just as he'd done with blue herons and kestrels.

Standing on the sidewalk in front of the building he'd photographed, Barnaby eventually realized he stood out and might be noticed by the Asian gentleman if he suddenly came out. He looked across the street and noticed the coffee shop where Zoot and his partner were sitting. He crossed the street and went in. Noticing that all the window seats were taken and that the view from other tables and booths would be inadequate, he quickly left and headed down the block toward Park Avenue South to a spot that gave him a more discreet point of view.

"Is he playing with us?" Zoot asked after Barnaby left the cafe.

"Looked right at us," Plummy said. "Maybe he was warning us off."

Zoot craned his neck to follow Barnaby's path down the block.

"He's stopped right next to our truck! He is playing with us."

"CIA?"

"No idea, but we're gonna find out."

Zoot called the agents in the truck and told one of them, a man named Urbanski, to follow Barnaby after he left the area. Barnaby stood watch for about an hour, and, in need of a bathroom break, he broke off and eventually found a coffee shop. He bought a small cup of the bean of the day — Guatemalan — and used the rest room. Urbanski, a balding, stolid special agent whose grandfather had suffered at the hands of a communist regime in Eastern Europe, came in behind him and jotted down notes on his target in his official bureau notebook: "Subject buys coffee. Uses men's room. Meeting someone inside? Dropping off message? Picking one up?"

Bladder relieved, Barnaby left the coffee shop and decided he might have missed the Asian man coming out of his building and that a return to his surveillance post might be a waste of time. Lesson learned, he wrote in his notebook: "watch from vantage point with quick bathroom access."

What he already knew from past observances was that the Asian man would be taking a train home at rush hour. Barnaby decided to try to pick up his trail that way. With time to kill before then, he pulled out the number of the accountant Jackie's building manager had provided and called him. Angelo said he could see Barnaby but not until the next day.

"I could give you a few minutes in the afternoon if you can meet me at a job site. You know where the fish market is?"

"Fulton Street?" Barnaby asked.

"No, no. They moved it a while back. It's in the Bronx"

Angelo gave him the name of a vendor who was one of his clients. Barnaby said he'd locate it on Mapquest, a search Tesla had taught him.

Rush hour was still a couple of hours away, so Barnaby bought some supplies he might need for his new consulting business: paper folders, plastic report covers, a personal version of Power Point to replace the one he'd had to give up when he left Montgomery & Co. And some Rollerball pens. A little treat.

He also bought a metal clickable counter of the type he'd seen Metro North employees use to tally the number of passengers on a given train. In watching for the Asian gentlemen, he thought the prop might provide a good cover. He'd noticed the railroad people counting over the years yet couldn't really recall what any of them looked like. He hoped the Asian gentleman would have a similar reaction.

He went over to Times Square and had lunch at Olive Garden, opting for the unlimited pasta entrée. It seemed the smart choice, though he wound up eating only one bowlful. He killed some time at a photo museum near Grand Central and got to the terminal about 4:30 p.m.

He got a schedule from the main kiosk and assumed his undercover pose, clicking away like a real railroad worker. As each train left with no sign of the Asian gentleman, he switched to a different track and began his surveillance anew. Around 5:30, he spotted his subject and followed him to a car that was third from the south end of the train.

The Asian gentleman, who read a report the entire trip home, got off at Tarrytown, and Barnaby followed him. The man got into a late model Mercedes. Barnaby took a quick photo of the back of the car and captured the license plate, but he realized he had no way of following the man. With plenty of cash in his pockets, he sprinted to a cab waiting at the station and told the driver to follow Jackie's car. The driver looked at him and said, "You mean like in the movies?"

"Yes."

The driver, a lanky man in his late 30s, took off in pursuit. After a couple of blocks, he asked if Barnaby was a detective.

"Not exactly."

"A G-man?"

"I can't really say."

The driver nodded as he looked at Barnaby in the rear-view mirror and said: "Gotcha."

The Asian gentleman didn't go far, turning left off Route 9 onto a side street in the village of Sleepy Hollow, just past the site of the long-abandoned General Motors automobile plant.

"Just drive by. I don't want him to think I'm following him."

"Right," said the driver, whose name was Earl.

At the end of the street, the driver asked for instructions, and Barnaby told him to go back to the station. He knew he could have taken Earl's cab home, but rates were very steep from village to village and his monthly ticket gave him a ride home that he'd already paid for. It was the smart move. At the station, Barnaby paid Earl and gave him a nice tip. Earl gave him a business card.

"You need me for any more jobs, any time day or night, you call me. I'll give you a good rate."

"That's very nice of you."

"Always wanted to be a shamus. I watch all those shows. Columbo reruns and all the CSIs. Maybe I could learn a thing from you. You know, pick up some tips."

Barnaby smiled at the misunderstanding and said, "I'll keep you in mind."

* * *

Back at the station, on a city-bound platform, Special Agent Urbanski, who hadn't managed to get a cab in time to follow Barnaby, had given up and was headed back to New York when he spotted Barnaby on the northbound platform. A train was just pulling in, heading north, and it quickly obscured Urbanski's view of Barnaby. He sprinted toward Barnaby's platform in hopes of following him. Before he got there through a series of stairs, the train had pulled out, leaving a breathless Urbanski watching its lights grow dimmer as it trundled north.

After he caught his breath, Urbanski called Zoot on his cell.

"The guy's definitely a pro. I lost him when he left the station here in Tarrytown, then when I picked him up, he arrived just in time to catch a train before I could get on it. You know, French Connection style."

"You figure out what he did in Tarrytown?"

"No, but he took a cab, and I got the number. I'll talk to the driver."

Urbanski saw another cab from the same company in the parking lot. He identified himself and said he needed to ask the driver of Cab 102 some questions about a passenger.

"That would be Earl."

The other driver wrote down Earl's cell number on the back of a receipt form.

"Good luck. He's little quirky."

"Quirky?"

"Well, like he always cleans the inside of his cab with Handy Wipes. Every surface. And sometimes he won't take certain people. Says they're not right for him."

"Is he otherwise reliable?"

"Earl?"

"Yes."

"Guess so. Only known him ten years."

Urbanski called Earl and identified himself. He described Barnaby.

"Oh, you mean the G-man."

"He said he worked for the government?"

"Not in so many words. But, you know, wink wink, nudge, nudge. I got the picture."

"Did he show you any credentials?"

"Nope...but then neither have you."

Urbanski gave Earl a pained smile.

"Can you tell me what he did?"

"Don't you G-men talk to each other?"

"I'm not sure he is a G-man."

"Then you're not sure he's not. Right?"

Urbanski had to admit he didn't know what to think about Barnaby, but he kept that to himself.

"Let's just forget him for now. I'll check him out, but it would help if I knew where he went after he left the station. We might be working on something similar, and I could help him out."

Earl paused, then said, "I suppose you could hire me and I could take you for a drive."

Earl drove Urbanski on the route he'd taken with Barnaby, turning left onto the same side street.

"There's the Mercedes we followed," Earl said. "That's the guy's house. The one with the black door."

Urbanski wrote down the address and the car's tag number.

"And he didn't talk to him?"

"Nope. Didn't want the guy to know he was following him, so we just went back to the station."

Earl did the same with Urbanski, who caught a train back to the city. He pulled out his government-issue Blackberry and sent Zoot a secure e-mail with the details. After a check of the address, Zoot e-mailed back: "Address is listed to a John Lin."

The man whose name turned out to be Lin was a relatively new person of interest in the bureau's surveillance of a counterfeit goods operation that did most of its business on Canal Street. He had been just Pirate10 to them. They hadn't known his name or where he lived. Suddenly they did, thanks to their following the irritating little man who had stumbled into their case.

The next day, Barnaby had the morning free as he waited to meet Angelo at the fish market. He took an early train to the city and walked to the coffee shop across from Jackie's building. He got a seat in the window, right where Zoot and Plummy had been sitting the day before. With some lessons learned on Day One, he'd come prepared for a lengthy stakeout, having brought a change of jacket, a ham sandwich, a bag of chips, a bottle of water, his MP3 player, small binoculars, a snack-size package of Oreos and $500 in 20s plus $10 in singles.

He plugged in his ear buds and scrolled through his selections of songs, looking for an appropriate one for launching his new business. Thanks to Tesla, he saw everything from old-school rap to Adele, but it was a selection from the Broadway show Pajama Game that caught his eye as he scrolled through the alphabetical list. He'd seen a revival with Gwyn when she was alive. This one stuck in his memory because it dealt with his profession.

He pressed Play, and from the original cast recording, he suddenly heard Eddie Foy proclaiming proudly in rhyme that he was "a time study man" and that wasting time was a crime. Barnaby didn't let the tick, tick tock of the factory clock rule him as Eddie Foy's character did. But he was punctual by habit and appreciated the song's jokes about how time-study men slept in their clothes to save time getting dressed in the morning.

A funny song, but, given the wrinkled suits that approach would produce, Barnaby knew it wasn't really the smart move.

*   *   *

When Zoot and Plummy arrived for another day of stakeout at the coffee shop, they found Barnaby seated at the table they'd used the day before. Zoot, in the lead, tried not to show any reaction. He walked past Barnaby without saying anything and went through an interior side door that led to a lobby and offices above the shop. With Plummy in tow, he climbed the stairs to the first floor and used a security card to open a door that said "Black and Johnson, Attorneys at Law." Inside was the night crew of his surveillance team, two male agents named Malone and Ortega.

"Anything?" Zoot asked.

"One visitor about 2 a.m.," Malone said. "Another new guy. Had a big duffel bag stuffed with something. Chinese looking. Got a shot of him coming out about half an hour later. Added it to the mug book."

"You notice a short guy this morning hanging around? Zip-up navy jacket and khakis. Got a knapsack. Sitting down in the coffee shop right now."

Malone shook his head.

"Not from here, but then we can't see straight down to the coffee shop," Malone said. A pause. "Chinese?"

"Definitely not," Plummy said. "Whitest guy you ever saw."

"Ah, I think I know the guy you mean," Malone said. "Saw him yesterday out front of the building. Figured he was just some goof."

"May not be a goof," Zoot said. "Whatever he is, he's back today looking at our perps, so makes me wonder."

"Maybe he works for some other agency," Plummy said.

"Urbanski says that's a possibility based on what he heard yesterday."

"Wouldn't we get a courtesy call on that?" Ortega said.

"How long you been doing this, Ortega?" Zoot asked.

"Nine months."

"In all that time, did you ever get a heads-up call from DEA, ICE, CIA, NSA?"

"Nope."

"And you never will."

"Unless they're ordered to call us, like for some multi-agency photo-op the U.S. attorney wants," Plummy said.

Zoot gave Plummy an irritated look.

"I stand corrected. Photos ops aside, they don't want us to know what they're doing."

"Can't be working for the D.A.," Malone said. "They left this one to us. They don't have the manpower after the budget cuts."

"Pirate10 is on the move," Ortega interrupted.

All four agents looked out the window and saw the man who called himself Mr. Lin. Plummy spoke into a radio mic that ran from her wrist to a unit strapped to the back of her pants-suit belt.

"Jimmy, Pirate10 on the move. Headed your way."

"Got him," Special Agent James Kotowski said from his surveillance van down the street. "Dressed nattily in black as usual. My guess is he's headed to Canal Street."

"You see anyone following him?"

"Just a guy in a blue jacket and tan pants," Kotowski said. "New perp?"

"Hmm," Zoot said. "Hadn't thought of that."

* * *

At Park Avenue South, Pirate10 hailed a cab. Barnaby, made note of the number and hailed his own taxi, excited at the prospect of the chase.

"Follow that cab, please," he told the driver, who was wearing a Sikh turban. "Which cab?" the driver asked.

Barnaby gave him the number, and the driver shot south down Park.

"Why do you want to follow that cab?" the driver asked.

Barnaby shrugged.

"Just curious. I want to see where that fellow is going."

"Do you know him?"

"No." Barnaby hesitated before saying more but decided to share a little of his new game. "It's sort of a hobby. I follow people to see where they go and what they do when they get there."

The driver ran a yellow light to keep up with the cab he was following. Through the intersection, he shouted back over his shoulder: "People don't like other people poking into their private lives."

"I'm just observing. I don't plan on getting involved."

*　*　*

Pirate10's cab did go to the Canal Street area, where the man went into a building that had purses, wallets and other leather goods on display out front on tables set up on the sidewalk. With the man inside, Barnaby again found himself in front of a building with no apparent purpose to explain if anyone asked. But he got lucky and had one provided.

"You like Gucci, Hermes?" a woman behind one table asked, smiling. "We have best prices."

She was dressed in jeans and a gray zip-up hoodie over a black T-shirt with a red Asian ideograph on it. Barnaby looked at the goods, all of which seemed well-made. He picked up a tan purse with a gold clasp, snapped it open and saw a label that said "Guccy."

"This isn't a real Gucci, is it?" he asked. "That's not how you spell it."

The woman shrugged.

"It looks pretty good for the price. You want the real look, that costs more." She looked both ways down the sidewalk. "You want to see?" The woman gestured toward the door of the building. Barnaby nodded at the opportunity to go inside and said brightly, "Yes, please."

The woman stopped Barnaby at the door by putting her hand on his chest.

"You're not the police, are you?"

Barnaby look taken aback.

"No. Just shopping. Got some very nice cologne yesterday up near Madison Square." He winked. "Wholesale."

The woman smiled and showed Barnaby inside. She opened a door on the right of the main hallway. On the far wall was a row of bookcases that covered most of the area. The woman went to the right of the unit, pulled it out a few inches and pushed it to the left, revealing a long cavern of purses and other luxury goods. The woman invited Barnaby inside and quickly located a purse identical to the one he'd examined. Rummaging through a box, she located what appeared to be a genuine Gucci clasp and a label with the name spelled correctly.

"If you want, after you buy it, I can put them together," she said. "Legally I'm not selling Gucci unless it's all assembled."

Barnaby took that in.

"Very clever."

The woman smiled. Barnaby asked the price, which was more than a thousand dollars.

"Wow! For a copy?"

"Our workmanship is as good as theirs. Maybe better, and the real thing will cost you three times that."

"Well, I didn't bring that much with me," Barnaby said.

"We take Visa or Master Card."

"Oh, I hardly ever use them. Too tempting. Maybe I could come back."

The woman flashed an irritated look.

"I'll be here all week," she said.

"Good. I was looking for something for my wife, and I want it to be special."

Barnaby was surprised how easily the lie had come. On reflection, he felt pleased with his new tradecraft.

"If you come back, ask for me. Jasmine."

The woman handed Barnaby a business card. The name on it read Jasmine Leung. No company name was indicated. The woman started to show Barnaby out when the Asian-looking man he'd been following came through the door. He took a long look at Barnaby and said to the woman in English, "I'm finished here. See you Friday."

"Very good, John."

John. Jackie. Good guess, Barnaby said to himself. And I know not only where he lives but where he'll be Friday.

From inside an FBI surveillance truck, a digital SLR camera with a telephoto lens snapped as the man left the building. Another click caught Barnaby and the woman right behind him, shaking hands.

Kotowski radioed the events to Zoot and Plummy, who'd remained at the phony-law-office command post.

"We need to find out who that is," Plummy said to Zoot. "He's either working with them or he's managed somehow to penetrate the gang for someone."

"If he's done that, and they figure it out, he's the one who'll get penetrated."

Chapter 5

The man Barnaby had followed had arrived by cab but chose to walk after leaving the Canal Street store. Barnaby followed at a distance until the man went down an entrance to the subway. Barnaby quickened his pace, pulling out his wallet as he did. He smiled as he located his Metrocard, which he kept stocked with rides in case he needed to visit clients of Montgomery & Co. He'd found they appreciated not being charged for cab rides as part of his time-and-motion service.

He spotted the man on the uptown platform, just a few feet north of the turnstiles. Barnaby swiped his card, noting he still had $20 left in rides. He turned quickly to the left in case his quarry turned around and might recognize him as the customer from Canal Street. Just in case, he did a quick change of hats and jacket, using a fat lady to block his costume change.

The man got off at 59th Street. Barnaby, at the other end of the car, followed him as he came up to the surface and walked west to Central Park. The man bought a Daily News from a corner newsstand and sat on a park bench near the zoo for a while. Barnaby took out his camera and his birder journal. Central Park, home to a dizzying variety of birds from wood warblers to red hawks, proved a useful site for Barnaby to observe his subject with plausible cover. Barnaby took some photos of common sparrows and even a flock of pigeons near the bench on which the man sat. Barnaby's wide-angle lens gave him a way to photograph John on the far end of his photo frames without seeming to be interested in him.

John was eventually joined by another Asian-looking man, though the two did not speak. Barnaby took a photo of the two men on the bench, this time pretending to be interested in the trees above them while capturing their faces at the bottom of his picture. He took out his journal and recorded a sparrow sighting just in case. He smiled, pleased with the cover story he was creating. Very Sherlock, he thought.

After a few minutes, the man the Canal Street sales woman had called John got up, leaving his newspaper on the bench. Barnaby started to follow him and noticed that the second Asian gentleman scooped up the newspaper and began flipping through it. That piqued Barnaby's interest, but he decided to stick with John because the other man was not a commuter and so didn't fit within the loose rules of his new game. Still, the newspaper thing made him curious.

Barnaby had to pick up his pace to catch up with John, who headed out of the park at an exit that led to Fifth Avenue. He walked by the second Asian man, who was still seated on the bench. Though Barnaby didn't see it, the second Asian man, pulled out his cell phone and made a call, watching Barnaby walk away as he did.

On Fifth Avenue, Barnaby saw John get into a cab and head south. He tried to hail a taxi to follow him as he had before, but none was immediately available, and there was not even a bus in sight. All Barnaby had for his efforts was the cab's number, which he recorded in a notebook with the time, date and place of the encounter. Another lesson learned: surveillance works better with a team and probably a car. Perhaps a cab hired for the day. Maybe Earl.

Barnaby considered going back to what he assumed was John's office in the wholesale perfume district, but he couldn't see what he might learn of interest from another stakeout at the coffee shop. For that matter, what was it he wanted to learn about any of the commuters he might follow? When was enough enough? Birds that he'd seen hundreds of times didn't interest him much any more. When would John become boring? Should he monitor his Sleepy Hollow home? Some danger there. He might be arrested as a Peeping Tom. His birder ruse probably wouldn't work with the police if he were just sitting in his car or Earl's taxicab down the block.

Maybe it was time to follow Commuter No. 2, whoever that might turn out to be. If he got another chance to observe John later, he could do that. He never mastered everything about a new bird species in a day or two of observations. And as he'd said before: why should humans be any different?

As for that day, he had an appointment with Angelo the accountant in the afternoon to discuss possible office sites and other aspects of his nascent consulting business. He needed to think about that for a while. He would have lunch somewhere and make up a list of goals — and maybe some core principles, as the management types at Montgomery & Co. were fond of saying

As he walked through Midtown looking for a restaurant with reasonable prices, he himself had become a subject of observation. Two completely different Asian men were following him. One was making his own notes on what was happening. The other was adjusting the 9-mm pistol in his shoulder holster. Watching them all was Special Agent Urbanski, who had been taking his pictures of everyone with a telephoto lens from behind a hot-dog stand, whose owner had been cooperative in providing cover after being given a $10 bill for one of his finest.

Urbanski followed Barnaby and his two Asian followers to a small burger place in the 60s and called in his findings to Zoot.

"He's either not as good as we think because he's being followed and doesn't realize it or he's really good because he's got Asians as his backup," Urbanski said.

"Let's not rule either out till we see your photos."

"E-mail me what you got, and we'll see if we can figure out who those guys are."

*　*　*

After a lunch of a hamburger, fries and an iced tea, Barnaby walked off a bit of his food by heading north on Lexington to catch a No. 6 train to the fish market in Hunts Point for his appointment with Angelo. Before Barnaby got to the subway entrance, a Chinese-looking man, engrossed in sending a text on his mobile phone ran into him. Barnaby stopped short on impact, and the person behind him bumped into his back. The Chinese man, whose black eyes popped out through his rimless glasses, uttered a quick "Sorry" and was on his way before Barnaby could say anything. When Barnaby turned to apologize the person behind him, there was no one there.

He thought nothing about it until he got to the subway entrance and went for his wallet to get his Metrocard. It wasn't there. Fortunately his practice was to keep his cash in his front pants pockets, so he was able to buy another Metrocard and make it to his appointment on time. But it would be a bother to have to replace his driver's license and monthly commuter pass, not to mention his wallet, which had been a gift from his wife.

He retraced in his mind where he might have lost it. He ruled out the restaurant, where'd he'd paid for lunch with his cash. He'd obviously had had it on the subway he'd taken from Canal Street to Central Park. Maybe someone had picked his pocket during the ride. Subways were infamous for that, Barnaby reminded himself.

He thought about retracing his steps that day to see if it might have fallen out of his pocket at some point, but he decided it wasn't very realistic to think that someone who had found it would contact him or turn it in to the MTA lost-and-found. The good news, he realized, as the subway took off for the Bronx, was that he had photocopies of his IDs in a filing cabinet a home, a practice he and Gwen had observed for years. He also kept his ATM card at home, a safeguard so he wouldn't be tempted to splurge or buy anything expensive without giving it some thought. He could retrieve it and get more cash to live on, and while he applied for a replacement license, he could keep the photocopy with him as proof he had a valid license. He would, of course, have to buy a new wallet, and find a replacement wallet-size picture of Gwen. That was the most irritating thing of all.

Several blocks away, the two Chinese men, known at their consulate as Mr. Bo and Mr. Xi, were discussing the contents of Barnaby's wallet during a cell-phone call with a man who called himself John Lin. Lin, after a short taxi ride, had taken a circuitous walk to an apartment in the Upper East Side that served as his hide-away office while he was in the city. Lin was in the midst of looking over some designer clothing sketches that an associate had illegally acquired a few days before.

"His name is Barnaby Gilbert," Bo, the stockier of the two, told Lin. "We have his address in Ossining."

"Pay him a visit to see what he's up to."

"What if he's with the police or the FBI?"

"I don't really care. If we need to get rid of him, we will. Just make sure you don't leave any evidence of who we really work for."

*   *   *

New York's wholesale fish market had operated for almost two centuries near the Brooklyn Bridge in Manhattan before being relocated to the South Bronx both to give it needed space and to try to break the grip of organized crime. Things looked spacious to Barnaby when he arrived. Too spacious for his taste. Downright wasteful.

He followed the directions Angelo had given him and asked for Mr. Dragon, Angelo's client.

"Who's asking?" said one of two beefy men dressed in wool shirts with stained aprons about their ample midsections.

"Barnaby. Barnaby Gilbert. Angelo, his accountant, asked me to me him here."

"Barnaby? What the heck kind of name is that?" asked the other man, whose nickname was Crunch.

"Isn't that what they called that purple thing on that kids TV show?" the first man, whose name was Jake, asked.

"That was Barney," Barnaby said. "Barnaby is of Greek or maybe Aramaic origin."

"Ara-what?" the first man asked

"Aramaic. It was the language of Jesus Christ."

"Jesus? Christ, you ain't some kind of Jehovah's Witness or something, are you? We don't allow them around here. Bunch of pests."

"No. No. Nothing to do with them. I'm just here to see Angelo. He's going to give me some advice."

"Well, I got some advice for you," the second man said. "Don't piss off Victor, and don't stick around here too long after it's dark."

The two men laughed, and the first told Barnaby to head toward to the back of the vast building and look for a stairway that led to the office. The office was on sort of an interior second story that was built out from the back wall and supported by pillars that formed the borders of a storage space for skids. The stairs leading up to it were made of pine that bore the indents of work shoes that had trudged upward countless times in the years before Barnaby mounted them.

Victor was a much skinnier man than the two behemoths Barnaby had met at the entrance. In his 40s, he had a deeply tanned face topped by dark black hair combed back in a pompadour. He was sitting behind a scarred wooden desk. A man in a sport coat and slacks was seated to his right in a visitor's chair. The door was open and Barnaby tapped it lightly to catch the men's attention. Both looked at the rapping sound at the same time, and Barnaby said in a quiet tone: "Excuse me. I'm looking for Angelo."

Angelo gave Barnaby the once-over and said: "With you in a minute, Mr. Gilbert. Just wait in the warehouse, and I'll come down and get you."

"Yeah, knock yourself out," Victor added. "If you like fish stink, you've come to the right place."

Victor laughed at his own remark. Barnaby smiled a little and went back down the stairs. Amid all the forklifts, skids and other equipment of the warehouse, Barnaby's trained brain immediately began to record the inefficiencies. He took out his notebook and began jotting down his thoughts. Caught up in his calculations, he took out his camera and began taking a few pictures as he always did on a job.

"The fuck you doing?" he heard Victor shout from behind him as he came down the office stairs.

Barnaby turned calmly around and said, "This is a very inefficient use of space. I think you could probably rent some of it out or at least work faster in here."

"What are you — some kinda expert?"

"Matter of fact, he is," said Angelo, who was right behind Victor. "He's what they call a time-and-motion man. Been working for one of the big Manhattan management firms. Now he's stepping out on his own. I'm going to help him get situated."

Victor nodded and eventually replied, "So what do you charge?"

Barnaby hadn't thought about that. He knew what Montgomery & Co. would charge for his work, but those prices, usually by the project, would probably be too steep for the sort of clients he might get at the start.

"If you're interested, we could do something by the hour and see if you like the results and then go from there. Do you have other businesses?

Victor laughed.

"Yeah, but I'm not sure you want to know about them. Could be dangerous to your health."

Barnaby looked puzzled but got an idea. He had his two-year severance and money in the bank. He didn't immediately need a fee.

"How about if I do this job for free, and if you feel comfortable, I'll do the next one for money?"

"Free's good. Usually I have to use a little pressure to get something free."

Barnaby wasn't sure what that meant.

"Look," Victor continued, "why don't you come back day after tomorrow? Early if you can."

"My time is your time. That was a motto at my former company."

Victor put out his hand and crushed Barnaby's fingers in a shake to introduce himself formally.

"Victor," was all he said.

"Barnaby. Barnaby Gilbert. I'm still having my business cards made up, but you can check my references with my former employer."

"Nah. If Angelo says you're OK, that's enough. I operate on trust. Trust and loyalty. Especially loyalty."

Victor walked Barnaby and Angelo outside the warehouse and waved goodbye. The two got into Angelo's car and drove to a coffee shop not far away to discuss Barnaby's plans for his own business. Angelo took notes for a while and finally said that aside from an office, there were tax issues and marketing to be considered.

"At the beginning, I'd keep your office in your house because you're going to be going mainly to client sites so rent is just a waste of money. Get an answering service to take calls while you're out. I got one you can use. The gals will pretend to work for you and you'll seem more professional. Once you get several clients and hire some people, we can consider some space. Yonkers is nice. Cheap. Not so dangerous any more. And it has a nice little-guy image if you are pitching to small businesses to start."

"And the train stops there."

"That important?"

"Saves on gasoline. Commuting is the smart move."

Angelo nodded and said, "I suppose. I usually just drive."

Angelo paid the tab and told Barnaby that he'd be in touch.

"If Victor is satisfied with my work," Barnaby asked, "what sort of other operations does he have?"

Angelo hesitated before he answered.

"I'll leave it to Victor to tell you. Let's just say he's got some factories, and he's into the Internet. And he's sort of overseas."

*   *   *

Urbanski had trailed Barnaby to the fish market, taking photos of him, Victor and Angelo. He e-mailed them to Zoot and called his boss.

"See anybody familiar?" Urbanski asked.

"Yeah. Real familiar."

"Who?"

"Someone from the old days. Dropped out of sight for a while. I wondered what happened to him. He was a fringe guy but connected. Question is: what is our new best friend doing with him, and is there a connection between fish and counterfeit goods?"

"So maybe the little guy's not a secret agent — just a crook?"

"Don't know, but we're gonna find out. Set up surveillance. I want to know if he farts in the shower."

"First we gotta find out where he lives."

"That's what you'll be doing the rest of the day."

"You're not coming?"

"Got a meeting."

"Bureau stuff?"

"Personal."

Chapter 6

Zoot finished up some paperwork at the office and was heading out when he ran into his former boss, Clarence Foster, at the elevator. The two exchanged nervous looks. Foster had been responsible for booting Zoot out of organized crime into counterfeit goods. On the surface, it didn't create much of a flap inside the office. There was some overlap for the two units because gangsters were behind a lot of the millions of fake goods sold in the city.

Zoot's mob expertise was the official reason given for the transfer. He'd bring vital knowledge to his new unit, the memo announcing the change said. But Foster and Zoot knew he should have been kicked out of the bureau not just transferred. Use of an official computer to view porn – some really nasty porn – was not a cool thing to be caught doing. Only Zoot's long tenure at the bureau and his close friendship with Foster had saved his career.

"How's it going?" Foster asked after neither said anything for a while.

"Pretty good. We may soon rid the world of fake Gucci handbags if things break our way."

Foster flashed a thin smile.

"I'm feeling safer already."

Inside the elevator for the short ride down, there was an uncomfortable silence until Foster asked: "How those sessions going?"

Zoot tensed at the question.

"Fine. It's good to talk."

"Usually is." Foster paused then asked, "Talked to Emma yet?"

Zoot's eyes narrowed as he tried to contain his anger. He would have liked to have said "None of your damn business." But Zoot knew he'd made it Foster's business.

"Now's not the time. It'd just ruin her – and me."

"Sure. Sure. I shouldn't have asked. Just concerned."

"No problem. Matter of fact, I'm just headed to a session round the corner."

"Huh. Pretty convenient."

"Yeah. They got 'em all over. Like AA. Lots of people thinking about sex in New York. You'd be surprised."

Zoot walked north from the bureau office and entered a storefront church that had made its meeting room available to the organization Zoot had joined as part of Foster's deal not to fire him. There were about ten people in the room, an after-work crowd. He was happy he didn't recognize anyone he knew from the courts or city police. Eight of the people were men; two were women. Heck of a place to pick up hot women, Zoot joked to himself. But humor was the last thing on his mind.

The meeting organizer asked for volunteers to go first. Zoot shot up, wanting to get it over with. He strode to the podium, leaving his suit jacket on so as not to show his holstered pistol.

"Good evening ladies and gentleman," he began matter-of-factly. "My name is Zoot, and I am a sex addict."

"Hi, Zoot," the crowd answered back in unison as they would for each speaker that night.

Zoot chose to tell the story of how he got sucked into his addiction to hardcore Internet porn. He'd told it before. It was a safe story, and he knew talking about it wasn't doing a damn thing to help him stop. He was just going through the motions. He still had a secret laptop at home with "FBI" taped across the top so his wife wouldn't look inside. He hadn't used it in a couple of days, but that was more because he'd worked late and because Emma had wanted to watch a movie on cable one night.

Members had to say something at these meetings, and so he chose to tell the tale of busting an S&M operation that some mobsters in Harlem had going. Afterward, he'd spent a lot of time talking with a woman who was the S part of the equation. He pawed over the handcuffs, dog collars, vinyl head masks, chains, wooden stocks and other paraphernalia of the game, asking detailed questions about how they were used and more importantly about why people subjected themselves to such punishment.

"It's just the way some people are wired," she'd said. "It either clicks for you or it doesn't, and if it does, it can get pretty interesting."

About a week after the interview, Zoot found himself checking out porn websites after Googling a simple "porn websites" and getting an amazing number of results. Some things made him laugh — like the woman in Thailand who promised a 10-step program to enable him to "swallow my poo." Sex Addicts Anonymous provided a 12-step program just like Alcoholics Anonymous, but he was pretty sure the woman's 10 steps didn't involve relying on God or some superior force to solve his problems.

For about a week, Zoot delved into the dark world of porn, telling himself it was all part of the investigation. He tried that explanation with Foster when he got caught at the office looking at hogtied naked women. It had bought him a little time, but he knew there was an incriminating trail of porn surfing on his bureau computer. The second time he got caught, Foster investigated the matter and found the electronic trail of Zoot's visits to sites on bondage, public humiliation, golden showers and naked teenage girls. Seeing no way out, Zoot admitted what he'd done but claimed it was an aberration, an irresistible curiosity that had stemmed from the S&M bust. He promised never to do it again, and Foster let him go. But a week later Foster confronted him with a printout of his computer that showed he hadn't stopped at all.

Zoot turned in his computer, which Foster had the techs wipe clean. But he bought another one for use at home and told his wife it was bureau-issue. He signed up with SAA, as he'd promised Foster he would, but at home he remained fascinated with the variety of pornography he could find with the click of a mouse. There were domineering men giving women pleasure through various forms of pain. At the end of some of these videos, the women would often say it was all great fun, which made it seem more normal than it was. They gave it a feel of fantasy, a fantasy he had never imagined on his own before the dark online world had sucked him in.

Sometimes, he'd get popup ads offering him live sex chat with someone right in his neighborhood. It was clear the operators of these chat rooms could tell where he was located, which unnerved him. It also made him extremely cautious. He never accepted any such offer and never used his credit card for any of the pay services.

He hadn't connected with any of the taunting women hawking their wares on the Internet. Too dangerous, he decided, but he did turn to online classified offerings to see if some regular person out there might share his interests in sex. After a while he laughed at the idea that anyone doing what he was doing was "regular." And what was he doing? Was he just looking for a quick real-life thrill, cheating on his wife with someone who was looking for the same? At first he found everything sexual interested him, young and old, but young became more dominant as he explored the erotic world. Eventually he decided he was more of a voyeur than someone who wanted actual sex with strangers.

He was still having intercourse with Emma a couple of times a month. Looking at all the images of women on the Internet had prompted him to try to spice up his situation at home, but his suggestions that they try some sex play ended frostily. His wife told him to leave his handcuffs at the office.

As he rattled through his spiel to the SAA group, he found himself asking what his new obsession was really about. Looking at sexy pictures was pleasurable. But being in a forbidden zone seemed even more delectable. He would get erections but often just leave it at that, wondering what kind of sick fuck he'd become.

He'd begun having erotic dreams about his new partner. He knew that was perilous ground. If something developed with Plummy and blew up, Foster would likely learn of it and fire him, given the unofficial probation Zoot was already on. Dreams might lead to daytime fantasies, and that could turn radioactive. Initially he didn't find Plummy that attractive. She had a nice body, but she was about three inches taller than he was, a difference that usually put him off when it came to women. He felt uncomfortable not being the dominant one.

Except when she had a drink or two, Plummy, channeling her inner accountant, was completely professional in their job relationship. She didn't flirt, but she could get uncharacteristically giddy and even funny if she had a drink too many when they stopped somewhere to chill out after a grueling day. He'd heard about her drunken shouting match with her former boss and her punitive transfer. They were both on the misfit squad, kindred spirits of sorts, and maybe that was why she'd became a focus of his thinking.

He was struggling to put her out of his mind, just as he was trying unsuccessfully to pretend that his "FBI" computer wasn't really in the locked bottom drawer of his home office desk. As his rehab session ended that night, he found Plummy was still in his thoughts, and he called her.

She lived in a rent-controlled studio she'd acquired while going to college in the city. Zoot had dropped her off a couple of times but had never been inside. She was home when Zoot called and said he wanted to go over a plan to figure out what Barnaby Gilbert was up to. Plummy sounded drunk but told Zoot it was fine to drop by. When he got there, she answered the door dressed in a satin robe and fuzzy lippers.

"Sorry I didn't dress for the occasion," she said, a tumbler of scotch in hand. "Want a drink?"

Zoot said yes to be friendly but he just sipped as Plummy gulped. A bottle of Johnnie Walker on a nearby table was more than half empty. Plummy had pulled out the mattress from her hide-a-bed love seat and sat the edge of it, showing some leg as her robe fell to either side of her body. Zoot, seated in a matching chair, tried not to stare as he went through what they knew and didn't about Barnaby.

"I think we need to tap his phone for starters," he said.

"You think a judge will find probable cause?"

Zoot smiled.

"Not sure we need a judge. I'm just interested in the information at this point, not a criminal case that'll stick."

Plummy nodded a bit too energetically.

"Ballsy, but I like it."

Plummy got up from the couch and poured herself another drink. She held up the bottle as if to say: Need any more? Zoot was still finishing his first one and declined. Plummy chugged about half the scotch she'd poured and sat back down on the end of the mattress.

"I'm feeling goooood now," she said, flopping back on the mattress so that her body above her knees was prone.

A little more leg was showing in this position, and Zoot found himself wondering what if anything she was wearing underneath the robe. Was this what he'd been hoping for when he'd called Plummy? He wasn't sure sex with a half comatose FBI agent was what he'd had in mind and decided to change the subject.

"Can I use your bathroom?" he asked even though he felt no need to.

"Mi casa es su casa," Plummy said, slurring the Spanish as she lifted her left arm toward the bathroom.

Zoot closed the bathroom door and tossed the rest of his scotch down the sink. He sat on the toilet for a few minutes, then flushed it and washed his hands methodically. He splashed some water on his face, which he found hotter than normal. Toweled off, he went back into the studio and found Plummy asleep and snoring slightly. He gave her a few light slaps on the cheeks to waken her but she was out cold.

Zoot took her glass from her right hand and rinsed it out in her sink. He wasn't sure what to do at first. He decided he should just tuck her in and leave. He pulled back the covers on the right side of the bed after shifting Plummy a bit to the left. He took her slippers off and got onto the mattress so he could grab her under her arm pits and pull her toward her pillows. With some tugging, he managed to get her in the right position with her head on a pillow and her whole body on the mattress. In the process, her robe came open a bit more, and he saw she was wearing only panties underneath. He went around to the foot of the bed and stared down at her.

An idea came into his head, a temptation really. Something else in the forbidden zone. Before he tried it, he closed her robe and attempted to revive her one more time with slaps on the cheek. But she didn't stir. Feeling safe, he opened her robe again, this time farther, so he could see both breasts, which looked large even though flattened out in her prone position. He stood on the end of the mattress for several minutes, admiring his handiwork. He decided to kick things up a notch. He pulled her panties off and enjoyed Plummy's full-frontal view. He wished he were looking at Plummy's image online so it could be downloaded or accessed anytime. He suddenly realized he might be able to do just that.

He knew Plummy had a point-and-shoot camera that she sometimes brought along on stakeouts. Zoot looked through her studio and found it in her top dresser drawer. He checked to see what images she had on the camera's memory card and found it was empty. She'd probably downloaded whatever she'd shot the last time to her computer and erased the images on the card in the process. That's what he usually did.

Zoot walked back to the foot of her bed and took a couple of shots of Plummy as she was, semi-naked. Then he put her in a couple of poses, including one without her arms through the robe's sleeves. He rolled her over on her side and took some nude shots from behind. Satisfied with what he had, he put her panties back on, making sure the maker's label was in the back. He slipped Plummy back into her robe, cinching the tie after fully closing the two sides. He pulled the covers over her. He picked up the camera again and popped out the memory card. He put the camera back in the top dresser drawer after wiping his prints off it. The next time she used it, she'd be puzzled about where the memory card had gone, but among the possible answers he was pretty confident his name would not come up.

Zoot turned out all lights except the bathroom one and let himself out. He was home in about an hour. He'd earlier told Emma he had to work late, figuring his SAA meeting might drag on. She didn't complain about the hour and said she'd put some meatloaf in the microwave in case he wanted that. He heated it up and brought his plate into his den, saying he'd turn in as soon has he cleaned up a file.

He took out the laptop marked "FBI" and inserted the memory card. He downloaded the images of Plummy to a new folder he labeled "Special Agent," erasing the images from the card as he did. He put the card in an interior pocket of his wallet. If he got lucky, he might even be able to slip it into Plummy's purse or toss it on the top of her desk for her to find. He was at heart a risk taker, which is why fighting mobsters had appealed to him. Risks meant potential harm, but they also produced rewards. And, risks aside, that day had been a very rewarding one.

Chapter 7

Barnaby arrived home in late afternoon that same day, unaware that Special Agent Urbanski had followed him almost to his door. He fed Tesla's kingsnake and pulled Hortense out of her glass pen, putting her on an arm of his couch under a lit 100-watt bulb lamp. The python seemed to enjoy herself there, like a sunbather relishing a day at the beach.

Barnaby had made some whole-wheat pasta earlier in the week and put it in the microwave to revive it. He added some bottled tomato-basil sauce that had been rated best of the store-bought brands in a magazine story he'd read. He poured himself a glass of cabernet, which he kept fresh by using a pump device that created a vacuum in the bottle to prevent oxidation. For a wine drinker who only wanted a glass or two from a bottle at a time, it was the smart move.

If Barnaby had looked out his living-room window, he would have spotted Special Agent Urbanski, pretending to look through the real-estate ads of a shopper newspaper he'd picked up at the train station. Urbanski made note of the address number on Barnaby's mailbox and continued down the street, irritated to find it was an unmarked dead end. That meant he'd have to walk past Barnaby's house again on his way out rather than being able to slip out of the neighborhood quietly on the other end to report in. A dead-end street was also less than ideal for later surveillance because people who lived on it tended to know all their neighbors, so a strange car or van would stand out.

That insight apparently hadn't occurred to Mr. Bo and his partner Mr. Xi, who had parked their tinted-window van at the entrance to the street. Bo, the trained sniper of the two, had his Heckler & Koch police rifle on his lap as the two men watched Urbanski continue his charade with the newspaper.

"Shall we pay Mr. Gilbert a visit after this person leaves?" asked Bo, as he cleaned his round steel-frame glasses with the end of his silk tie.

Mr. Xi, dressed in a black suit over a gray shirt and black tie, used his binoculars to get a closer look at Urbanski.

"I have a bad feeling about him."

"What?"

"I smell somebody official. Maybe FBI. And where there is one, there's probably another close by."

"You think we've been spotted?"

"Let's not take a chance. John wouldn't want that. We can come back later. Mr. Gilbert's not going anywhere."

*   *   *

In the morning, Barnaby awoke at his usual time. He had the fleeting thought to sleep in because he could. He had no business appointments. But he invoked the carpe diem motto that J.J. Montgomery himself displayed on a sign on his office wall. He would seize the day by tracking another of his fellow commuters. He told himself it wouldn't be long before he'd be hip deep in customer demands and his new hobby would be relegated to weekends, when few commuted. This way, he'd jump start his new venture.

The night before, he'd set his coffee machine to begin brewing at his normal wake-up time, which was another reason to get out of bed. Coffee began turning bitter about 20 minutes after it was brewed, he'd learned in previous experiments, so if he slept late, he'd have to drink a bad cup or have to start over and waste the grounds. In a way, as Mr. J.J. Montgomery would say, alea jacta est, the die was cast the evening before when, subconsciously, he'd committed himself to getting up at the usual workday hour by putting the grounds in the machine.

He drank the hot, dark liquid — one sugar — from his favorite mug, which bore the faded decal of a bird sanctuary that he and his late wife had visited on a dream vacation in Costa Rica several years before. As he did, he gazed out the double kitchen window, which provided a seasonal view of the wide river as he stood at the sink. His eyes glimpsed the wash ropes Gwyneth had used to dry clothes in all but inclement weather. Partly because it was no longer a shared task, he'd chosen to do his sheets and pillow cases in the dryer after she died. That was more time efficient, but he found he missed the paper-crisp feeling and fresh-air fragrance of his bedclothes that Gwyn's old-fashioned method had produced.

His gaze ran toward the end of the cotton lines, and he noticed the wooden clothespins that he'd abandoned there since Gwyn had died. The orphaned fasteners made him think of her hanging out the sheets and pillowcases for their queen-size bed in the years when she'd been healthy. They'd decided queen was the right dimension for them, given their body sizes, the square footage of their bedroom and the comparative costs of mattress covers, duvets and the like.

Thinking of that bed, he was reminded that was where she'd spent most of her last weeks. And back came the images of lifting her from it more times that he cared to recall to take her to the bathroom and bathe her soiled body until she needed more professional help outside their home.

He made a daily effort to lock those painful memories far back in his mind. And yet a simple, unexpected encounter with clothespins had brought them rushing back. He made a mental note to bring them in from their lonely perch so it wouldn't happen again.

He had breakfast, which consisted of a piece of whole-wheat toast with orange marmalade — no butter — and a dry-oat cereal laced with skim milk and topped with banana slices. As he ate, he pushed Gwyn back into the recesses of his memory, using a number of tricks, some tried and true. At first he mentally replayed his last birding event at the point. Then he ran through the dream sequence of starting his own business with Victor as his initial client, followed by many imaginary others. Even his new hobby helped change the subject, generating a brief thrill as he considered his pursuit of the unknown. By the time he'd finished eating, he found he had a spring in his step as he walked toward the train station, speculating on who his next quarry might be.

As the train pulled out of Tarrytown, Barnaby didn't see John, so he scanned the car for other regulars. There was the bickering family at one end. In the middle of the car, sat the big bluff, bald man who wore the Burberry trench coat. As the man always did, he took off his topcoat and folded it very carefully before putting it in the grated overhead rack. Then he sat down and read his papers by folding them in half vertically so as not to bother anyone who sat next to him.

The hennaed-haired woman he'd nicknamed Helga was there too. She was speaking French to another passenger a few rows in front of the bluff man. When she rode her three-speed bicycle to or from the station, she reminded Barnaby a bit of the actress Margaret Hamilton, who had scared the bejeezus out of Judy Garland in the black-and-white part of the Wizard of Oz as the angry neighbor who wanted Dorothy's dog Toto put down. But she was better looking than the actress and even a little sexy in a tightly-wound sort of way. Might she be a good catch, Barnaby wondered.

The young school girl was in jeans and a high-school letter jacket that day, sitting right in front of the henna-haired woman. Maybe school uniforms weren't mandatory or she had a day off. There was no school letter on the jacket, which was black with black leather arms. She had her red backpack again and was at a window seat on the land side of the train line.

She passed the 35-minute ride to 125th Street without looking out the window, instead bopping her head as she listened to her iPod. Occasionally her head would focus downward, and Barnaby imagined she was texting friends on her cell phone. Tesla had told Barnaby that young people preferred texting to e-mail even though you had to deal with thumbs and a distinctly inferior method of entering letters. Barnaby had done a test run of texting but decided it was not for him. Pressing a key multiple times to get the right letter was inefficient. He was still inclined to call people he knew rather than e-mail, but he accepted e-mail as part of modern life and had mastered its commands to help clients streamline their business operations. But no LOLs or WTFs for him. Just plain English.

Barnaby daydreamed during most of the trip south, having decided to pick his subject for the day as people poured out of the train at Grand Central, but he was startled out of his reverie by the sound of the schoolgirl's backpack hitting the train car floor as she climbed over a sleeping passenger next to her. He heard the girl shout "Asshole!" at the dozing man as she picked up her bag and headed for the exit. On a whim, he decided that he would follow her that day, intrigued by the unexpected swearword that had come from her youthful mouth.

Barnaby's seatmate was asleep too, and by the time he crawled over him and got into the aisle, several other passengers were between him and the girl in the exit line. Three were teenage boys who were eyeing her periodically over their shoulders. His guess was they all went to some private school in the city, even though the public schools of villages along the Hudson were rated quite well nationally, based on advance placement courses and median SAT scores. Public school seemed the smart choice, given the property taxes that parents were already paying. Tesla had gone to public school, and she was a genius, as far as Barnaby could tell.

Barnaby wondered if the schoolgirl would just be transferring to the subway to get somewhere or if she'd be walking through Harlem to her destination. Perhaps with all the redevelopment of the area he'd read about, it was safe enough to walk the streets in daylight. She might take a bus, he suddenly realized. Following her on a bus would be tricky. Mysteries and challenges. It was proving a fun morning.

Barnaby had nicknamed the girl Cate because her erect posture gave her a regal look like the actress Cate Blanchett playing an elf. As she left the train, she headed for the subway entrance on Lexington, as the boys did. But when they went toward the trains, she walked south, above ground. After about a block, she reached into a side pocket of her knapsack and pulled out a knife. Barnaby saw her press a button and a large steel blade fell downward. A fellow birder, a former Marine, had one like it. He called it a gravity knife. Barnaby was pretty sure it was illegal in New York.

Just after the first subway stop south of 125th, the girl turned left, with Barnaby about three-quarters of block behind her on the other side of the street. To have used the subway to get such a short distance would probably have taken her longer, given the waiting time. With her knife as ready protection, Barnaby calculated, the girl had probably made the smart move.

Barnaby had a baseball cap in his backpack and he put it on while stashing away his windbreaker to change his look. At the station, he had put his SLR camera around his neck and began taking pictures of some of the area's famous houses. That day his cover story was: Barnaby Gilbert, architecture buff. The zoom lens also gave him a chance to take some photos of the girl at a nice distance, though he was only able to get back and profile shots before she got to her destination, a brownstone on a block east of Lexington.

The house looked about a hundred years old and had been restored. As he walked by he noticed a brass sign to the right of a door buzzer. It said: "Visits by Appointment Only." Perhaps the girl had a doctor's appointment before school. As he had with John, Barnaby lurked down the street where he couldn't be seen from the front window of the renovated house.

By 10:30 a.m., nature called as it had during his stake-out of John's building. Barnaby found a pizza take-out place with a public bathroom. He used the facilities after buying a pepperoni slice that he put in his backpack in case he had to continue his surveillance during lunch. He returned to his spot down the block from the house. He looked with envy at the cars and vans that were parked on the street and longed for some sort of rolling headquarters for his observations, like the vans he and his friends used to track birds along the river. But stuck with a group of subjects who only traveled by train, he didn't see how that would ever be possible.

He could, of course, go where his subjects were likely to be, like going to George's Island, a known roosting area, to track eagles in winter. In this case, he could wait for his commuter colleagues to get off the train on their way home. Where they lived was part of their story. He decided that's what he would do with the young girl. That gave him some time in the afternoon to prepare for the visit to Victor's warehouse the next day. But first, as long as he was in the area, he decided to satisfy his curiosity about why the girl had gone into the house. He had his cover story, so he pressed the buzzer with some confidence. An elegantly dressed woman who looked of mixed race gave him a long stare before saying, "You lost, grandpa?"

Barnaby straightened his shoulders and responded: "I am not a grandfather, and I am not lost, but I do have an interest in your building. An architectural interest. And I wonder if I might take some photos for my collection."

The woman laughed and said, "Are you sure it's architecture you're interested in, honey?"

Barnaby was taken aback at her remark and responded, after a short delay: "Yes, I am."

"We got a our own little collection inside. But it'll cost you if you want to take their pictures."

Barnaby saw an opening.

"What kind of collection?" he asked.

The woman smiled.

"You mean to say you don't know what this place is?"

Barnaby shrugged.

"A doctor's office — or possibly a private school?"

The woman cackled.

"Well, sometimes people play doctor, and you could learn a thing or two, but officially it's neither of those."

A town car pulled up in front of the house and a well-dressed man in a double-breasted suit got out and told his driver to come back in an hour. He mounted the steps, shot Barnaby a quizzical look and said "Hello, Selma. I think I'm a little early."

"No worries. Top of the stairs. She's ready. The Blue Room, like last time."

Barnaby said nothing as the man pushed by him. After the man mounted the stairs, the woman finally said, "Time to go, Pops. If you figure out what you want, you came back. And bring your credit card."

She closed the door and Barnaby, feeling slightly angry at being summarily dismissed, went directly across the street and snapped some wide-angle shots of the building. To further enhance his cover, he went down the block and photographed some others. As he passed a white van with tinted windows, Special Agent James Cooper snapped Barnaby's picture and asked his partner: "Who's the guy with the Brownie?"

"No idea," an FBI agent named Rooney said. "But the guy in the town car is a hedge-fund manager. Lives in Connecticut. Comes here couple of times a month, one of our trackers says."

"What's the deal with him?"

"SEC's got a sudden interest. Seems to be very lucky making some recent trades. They asked us to check him out. Make sure he's not cheating."

"Guess we can report he started the day with a bang."

Both men laughed.

"Include the camera guy in the file, too?"

"Can't hurt. He might be working for her. He had a knapsack. Maybe he's a bagman."

* * *

After some more picture taking, Barnaby walked back to the 125th Street station and took a local back home. There, he did some outlining of a presentation for Victor. As rush hour approached, he stored his files and headed back to the station in his car, a low mileage Honda that had given him very little trouble, perhaps because he rarely drove it. If he had to follow some-one by car, he was ready.

About 5:30 p.m., he spotted the schoolgirl and got out of his car to follow her. She made a stop at a mini-deli. He could see from the front window that she was buying a soft drink and a bag of chips. She tossed the clerk some money, and some of the coins fell behind the counter. When the young man bent over to pick them up, the girl snatched a candy bar from the counter and stashed it in her jacket pocket. Barnaby was stunned to see such an innocent girl shoplifting. His state of mind was agitated enough that he wasn't as careful as he should have been in fol-lowing her after she left the store. He got too close, and after a few blocks, she turned back and confronted him, an unopened knife in her right hand.

"Stop following me, creep, or I'll cut you."

She pressed the knife's release button and the blade slid out. Barnaby sensed quickly the danger of the knife as well as that of being accused of molesting a young girl. He took a more aggres-sive approach in responding than he normally would have.

"Well, then I might have to say I followed you after you shoplifted at the mini-deli."

The girl's eyes narrowed.

"You better keep your mouth shut, if you know what's good for you. My dad has pals who'll kill you if you don't."

Barnaby's eyes blinked.

"I have no intention of informing on you. I, I was just trying to protect myself."

"The fuck you talking about?"

Barnaby took in a breath and let it out before he responded.

"If you told the police I was following you, that might not be good for me, even though my intentions are completely hon-

orable. I was just trying to discourage you from reporting anything."

The girl looked at Barnaby a moment, then said, "Yeah, sure.
Honorable. Like you don't want to get in my pants."

"That is not my intention. I was just trying to see where you
go."

"Right."

"Really. It's just a hobby...I'm a bit of a bird watcher, a
birder, and I decided — on a bit of lark really." Barnaby paused
after that remark. "Oh, sorry, no pun intended."

The girl rolled her eyes.

"Anyway, I wanted to see if I could find out more about people who take my train in the morning or afternoon."

"That's where I've seen you!"

"Yes. You usually take a window seat, on the land side. You
listen to music and text your friends during the ride. At least that
is what I have observed."

"You're a stalker!"

Barnaby looked shocked at the accusation.

"Absolutely not. I'm interested in men too."

"So you're like gay?"

"No!"

"So what then? Bi?"

"Bi what?"

"Bisexual, you moron."

"No, no, no. Not that either. I'm just curious, as I'm sure a
lot of passengers on that train are about fellow riders. Didn't
you ever wonder about all those people you see every day?"

"Earth to crazy person: just leave me out of your fantasy —
unless you're willing to pay, of course.

"Pay?"

"For sex. Isn't that what we're really talking about?"

"Of course not. You're just a girl."

The girl laughed.

"Yeah, like that stops guys."

"I assure you...."

"Cut the shit, Bozo, and let's get one thing clear. Most I do is a BJ, and usually not that. For someone like you, lap dance is more likely. No exchange of bodily flues."

"A BJ?"

The girl let out a blast of air from her lungs in exasperation and walked off at a forced-march pace. After about a dozen steps, she yelled back over he shoulder: "Just get some fuckin' money, and in the meantime, don't follow me anymore. I got a knife, and I know how to use it."

Barnaby went back to the station parking lot, got his car and drove home. He had picked up his mail from the black metal box at the foot of his driveway and had the envelopes and catalogues in hand as he opened his front door. Once in, someone grabbed him from behind, and a man, the same Chinese-looking man who'd bumped into him, he thought, punched him in the stomach. Barnaby had the air knocked out of him and had trouble breathing for a while. As he tried to recover, the man behind him shouted in his ear: "Why are you taking pictures of Mr. Lin?"

Barnaby was barely able to respond but managed to wheeze out: "I don't know any Mr. Lin."

Mr. Bo, the man who had punched Barnaby, kicked him in the ribs and shouted: "Liar! You have his pictures on your computer."

The penny finally dropped.

"You mean, John?"

"Yes. John Lin. What is your interest?"

Barnaby found himself again explaining his seemingly harmless hobby to another angry audience.

"Just a hobby. I follow people on my train to see what they do. It's like bird watching."

"Do you think we're idiots?" Mr. Xi asked.

"It's the truth. I didn't even know his name was Lin till you told me."

"But you knew his first name."

"Yes. I heard someone call him that at a Canal Street store."

"Ah! So you admit you were following him?"

"Of course. That's what I said."

"Who are you working for?" Mr. Xi asked?

"No one. I'm self-employed."

Xi's face turned red as blood surged to his face. He twirled and kicked Barnaby in the head and gave him a karate chop to the back of the neck. Barnaby fell to the floor unconscious. Xi checked Barnaby's pulse.

"He's still breathing. You're losing your touch."

"Maybe we should finish him off."

"No. We were just supposed to send him a message. We've done that, but before we kill him, we'd better get authorization."

Xi reached into his jacket pocket and took out Barnaby's wallet. He proceeded to rip up most of its contents as he stood over Barnaby's body. The plastic driver's license proved more difficult. Xi used a switchblade to cut it into quarters.

Bo laughed at his partner's theatrics.

"Feel better?"

The two men left, leaving the front door slightly ajar. An hour later, Barnaby came to, feeling groggy and unable to stand. He crawled to his bedroom phone and called Tesla. She came over about 15 minutes later, entering cautiously. Dressed in black jeans, a matching T-shirt and a charcoal hoodie, she ran her fingers through her short blond hair as she surveyed the scene. She looked puzzled when she didn't find Barnaby in his den or the kitchen.

"Geez-us, Mr. G. What happened?" she finally said after spotting Barnaby lying on the floor next to his bed.

Barnaby filled Tesla in. She said he should call an ambulance to take him to her mom's emergency room, the closest in the area. Barnaby put her off, saying he just wanted to collect himself first. An ambulance seemed too much fuss, he said. Tesla helped him onto his bed and had him go over the details of the attack one more time.

"They looked in your computer?" she asked at one point.

"That's what they said. They saw a picture I took of him."

"Not good. It may mean nothing, but those Chinese are champion hackers. They may have left you a nasty surprise. I can run some diagnostics. But to be totally sure, I think I should take it to a friend of mine who has a cyber-security firm. She used to work for the government."

"Whatever you think best, but I do need a computer to help me with my new business."

"I think I can get a loaner from her. Good thing I stored all your files on the remote server, so we can download everything from there without any worries that it's infected."

Tesla brought up the idea of the emergency room again, but Barnaby still said no. She had learned a few first-aid basics from her mother. As a compromise, after examining Barnaby's head, she went to his guest bathroom and wetted a hand towel with hot water. He wasn't bleeding, but she cleaned up the surface around the slight wound on his head. She got some ice cubes from the refrigerator and put them in a zip-top plastic bag so Barnaby could apply the compress to the bump on the side of his forehead where his attacker's shoe had landed.

"You should really have a doctor check your head, Mr. G. Could be a concussion. I'll drive you myself, if you want. Got my license back."

Barnaby finally gave in.

"Probably best. Mine's all ripped up," he said.

Tesla drove up Route 9 to the emergency room. Having lost her driving privileges for speeding at the beginning of the year, she kept strictly to the limit to the annoyance of some light-flashing drivers behind her. The hospital, which had a view of the Hudson for those who cared to notice, wasn't very crowded at that time of the evening. There was only one car accident victim and no one complaining of injuries related to drinking or spousal abuse.

The doctor who treated Barnaby, a woman in her late 20s, recommended an MRI, which was done in a separate building. By the time she had patched Barnaby up, given him some painkillers and ruled out a concussion, it was after nine.

"Did you report this to the police?" the doctor asked.

"No. I just came here."

"Well, you should."

Barnaby promised he would, but the only thing he wanted to do was to go home and climb into bed. He filled out the rest of the insurance forms first. The only good news that night was his realization that the bills would be honored by Montgomery & Co.'s insurance provider, according to his severance deal.

Back in the reception area, Barnaby found Tesla playing with his little camera, which she'd brought along to see if the attackers had done anything to it. She went through the settings and finally reviewed the photos on the memory chip. She saw the ones of John Lin, an office building with export company names on the windows, Lin with another man on a park bench and several shots of a young woman with spiky white hair. Tesla's eyebrows went up on seeing the last ones. She held up the final shot and asked: "What's with you and Dora Pivo, Mr. G?"

Barnaby was confused at first.

"If you mean the student, I don't know her name. I was just taking some photos."

"Well, it was Pivo-something but her dad made her officially shorten it to Pivo after he went to the slammer."

"He's in prison?"

"Yeah. Sing Sing. That's why she moved here. So she could visit him."

"You know her?"

"She was in my class for sophomore year, but she dropped out when she was a junior. Didn't want to go to school, and when she turned 16 they couldn't make her. Word is her dad got her some job. In the city."

Barnaby nodded as he took that in.

"What was he convicted of?"

"Some hacking thing. He and some Ukrainians were making millions. The police tricked him into coming to the U.S. and grabbed him. It was in the local paper."

Barnaby nodded and then asked, in a complete change of subject: "Do you know what a BJ is?"

Tesla laughed out loud.

"Since about the 4th grade. Why?"

"Nothing really. It just came up recently."

Tesla looked at Barnaby.

"With Dora?"

Barnaby cleared his throat.

"Let's say yes."

"She offered you a blow job?"

Barnaby made the abbreviation connection.

"Not exactly."

"I'm impressed, Mr. G. Every guy in my class was trying to do her — at least until her dad had somebody beat the crap out of one of them and that was that. She was radioactive. And then she dropped out." Tesla waited a moment then asked: "So did you get it?"

"What?"

"The BJ?"

"No. I just got a photo."

* * *

Barnaby woke the next morning with a headache and took an aspirin in addition to the painkiller he'd gotten at the emergency room. His face was black and bluish on part of one side, and it hurt to shave after he'd showered. He thought about staying in bed that morning, but he'd promised Victor he'd survey his warehouse, early if he could. He decided that canceling his appointment would be a bad way to start a new business. He fed Tesla's bullfrogs. They got some grasshoppers he'd bought from the local pet shop. He gave some cooked chicken to Fred, the snapping turtle. The snakes, snoozing in their separate glass containers, didn't need to be fed till the next day.

Tesla had persuaded Barnaby to let her python lounge out of its pen. He wasn't comfortable with the idea at first, but he caved in to her argument that Hortense wouldn't be slithering around the house to parts unknown because she wouldn't want to leave the warmth of the lamp they used to keep her in place. Still, when the snake was out sunning on the couch, Barnaby made it a habit to sit in the room's main arm chair, where he could keep an eye on her.

Pets fed, Barnaby calculated it would be cheaper to take public transportation to Hunts Point than to drive to meet Victor, but he didn't want people staring at his bruises on the train, so he decided to drive and wound up making better time. Before he left, he put his driver's license and train pass back together using some Scotch tape and laminated them with a machine he'd bought from a TV promotion.

It took Barnaby less time to drive to Victor's warehouse than it would have on public transportation, he calculated, and he arrived a bit early, though still in slight pain even after taking the pills. He told Crunch he had an appointment with Victor. Crunch, who was doing some arm lifts with free weights, made a call on his cell phone, and Barnaby was waved through.

Victor came down the office stairs as Barnaby was walking toward it.

"The fuck happened to you?" Victor said. "You look like somebody beat the crap out of you."

Barnaby smiled weakly.

"Somebody did."

"Who?"

"Some Asian guys. Chinese I think."

"Those Chinese guys know how to fight. You need to shoot 'em just to slow 'em down."

"I'll try to remember that for next time, though I don't own a gun."

Victor looked a Barnaby a moment, then said: "Maybe I can arrange something."

Victor didn't press Barnaby for details on the attack, so Barnaby got to work despite his condition. He took some pictures and some notes.

"I can see several inefficiencies right away," Barnaby said, "But let me do some more research here and online, and I'll send you a report. I'll need to do some interviews."

"Whoa. People don't like to answer too many questions around here. It's sort of a closed society."

"I just need some basics like how they determine prices and what costs are."

"Now you're getting into trade secrets. We don't tell anybody other than the buyer, one at a time, what we charge."

"That makes for a very inefficient market."

"And a very profitable one."

"Well, it would all be confidential. Maybe if you talked to your people, that would smooth the way. The buyers would never have to know."

"I thought it would be simpler than this."

"As the saying goes: 'No pain, no gain.'"

"My good-for-nothing son says: 'No pain, no pain.'"

Barnaby considered that alternative logically, not seeing it as a joke.

"That is also true, but no pain still means you don't gain anything."

Victor snorted a laugh.

"OK, but any word of this leaks out, and there will be consequences."

Barnaby smiled and said, "Of course. If I were indiscreet, you'd have every right to sue me."

"I was thinking of something a little faster than a lawsuit."

*   *   *

Barnaby spent the day interviewing Victor's dealers and the truckers who brought the fish from fishing boats to the market. He also tried to debrief some of the buyers, many of whom were Asian, but didn't get very far even with those who spoke perfect English. At the end of the day, he met again with Victor.

"It was a productive day. I'll work up something and bring it back to you."

"Great. If I like it, I got a couple of other businesses you might want to take a look at. For them, of course, I'll pay you something."

"If we get to that point, I'll draw up a contract. Or maybe I'll ask Angelo to do it."

"I usually just do handshake deals. And pay in cash."

"I can handle that, although it did occur to me, I don't actually know your full name, Victor."

Victor flashed a thin smile.

"Dragon. Vittorio Dragon. I got a couple a others I use for businesses purposes, but with you, I'm giving you the official one."

"Hmm. What kind of name is Dragon?"

"Could be a lot of things, but in my case my pop was Ukrainian. Well, Ukrainian-Italian, which is a heck of a combination. And my mom was from Naples, so that's where the Vittorio comes from. But Dragon comes in handy in business, you know."

"I'm not sure I follow you."

Victor's eyes narrowed.

"There's still a lot of anti-Italian bias out there. If you got a name with too many vowels in it, some people automatically think you're some kind of crook."

Chapter 8

As Barnaby tossed his notebook of interviews on the passenger seat and drove away from the fish market, Zoot and Agent Urbanski put their zoom-lens camera away and followed him, ending their coffee-laced stakeout.

"So either this guy is some kinda superagent, a crook or Woody Allen is going to play him in the sequel to 'Zelig.' He's everywhere."

"There's got to be some simple explanation."

"So how do we get it?"

"Keep following him. He'll make a mistake. And now we have the wiretap."

"Why not just grab him and sweat him?"

"At this point, he's still leading us to things and people we didn't know, people who may be working together, so let's play this hand for a while."

Instead of going straight home, Barnaby stopped at a Mexican place and treated himself to half a roasted chicken to go. It was a celebration of his first real day of his new business. He recognized that his revenue entry, if he'd been keeping score, was zero. But he felt confident about the future after closing his first sale, just like the Chinese man at the wholesale perfume store, and he was anticipating the good luck that was supposed to come with it.

Once home, he got some frozen green beans out of the refrigerator and was about to put them on the stove when he noticed the blinking light on his answering machine. He played the message and found Tesla had gotten a replacement computer for him from her cyber-security friend and that she could bring it over.

Tesla lived just down Barnaby's dead-end street, an environment she knew well, so it didn't take a surveillance genius to notice the unmarked FBI car with Zoot and Urbanski sitting in it, trying to look unobtrusive in their baseball caps and blue windbreakers as they listened to Barnaby's phone calls and recorded his visitors. Tesla slipped by them without showing any interest as she memorized the car's license plate number.

"Neighbor kid," Urbanski said. "Seems to come over regularly."

"Any perversion?"

"Like sex, you mean?"

"Not unheard of."

"The kid is 17 not 7."

"Just saying."

"Well, you want weird, the place if full of reptiles. He's got a huge snake coiled up under a reading lamp. Scared the crap out of me."

"Maybe he's running a cult. Like that guy in the Conan movie."

"All I know is he's weird, and it doesn't appear to be an act."

"We'll figure it out, now that we can monitor his calls. You put any bugs in his house?"

"No. Didn't think this was that serious."

"It suddenly is, so let's get that done ASAP in case he has some important conversation in there that he doesn't do on the phone. Like whatever he's saying to his little girlfriend about now."

What Tesla was doing was setting up the replacement computer by downloading the files she'd stored remotely.

"We can use this one for a while because my friend said she'd like to monitor yours for a while. It's part of a bot network, it turns out."

"A bot?"

"Yeah. A slave. Someone took over your computer and is using it without your permission."

"The Chinese?"

"Not absolutely sure, but it appears those guys who attacked you just went through your files based on entry dates. They didn't leave any malware or other bad stuff that my friend's company could find. But she did find your PC was part of a slave network they've been tracking for the last six months. The bad guys probably got you to open some e-mail a ways back and you were grabbed."

"I did have a birthday card a couple of months ago from someone name Willa, which was strange because I don't know any Willa."

"Did it arrive on your birthday?"

"Yes. That's why I opened it. It was quite an amusing little video card with songs and everything."

"There you go. All they needed to know was your birthday, which is easy, and send the card. You open it, and they can get into everything."

"But why?"

"Most want to get into your bank account. I'd check that right away and change your passwords, but they might just want to force your computer to visit websites to kite up the hits on the ads."

"Why?"

"They arrange contracts and get money for every hit. They send millions of customers who buy nothing. Nice for them. Sucks for the website."

"So what do I do?"

"Nothing right now. My friend will track the bad guys from your computer and shut them down and then cancel the slave instructions eventually. It'll take a while but it'll be good as new. In the meantime we have this nice Mac Air. It's awesome."

"Well, that was very nice of your friend."

"She has an ulterior motive. She wants me to work for the NSA and then come help her some day. She used to work there a while back. She knows everything about hacking. That's how we met. At a hacker's conference." Tesla smiled at the memory. "She said I was headed to the dark side."

"It all sounds a bit like some crime novel."

"Or spy novel, but it's pretty real, Mr. G."

Tesla finished with the computer and asked if there was time to play with the trains set downstairs. Barnaby had turned his basement into a model railroad network with tracks and switches and stations spread over a vast plywood table. Unlike kids who like to push locomotives to their maximum speeds, often derailing their trains, Barnaby, like other adult train enthusiasts, followed the schedules of famous and obscure trains, figuring out how to get from point A to B so that trains left and arrived precisely on time. To give him a vaster landscape to work with, Barnaby had scrapped his HO scale models and switched to an N version, which offered equipment that was 160:1 in scale to the real thing.

"So what's it going to be tonight, Tesla?"

"How about something in the 19th Century. Santa Fe maybe?"

Barnaby went to a shelf on the back side of the basement and searched through books of train schedules. He finally settled on one and flicked through its pages."

"We'll need to change the cars. Amtrak equipment won't do for 1875."

*　　*　　*

After an hour of play, Barnaby and Tesla put their 10-car train into the yard and switched off the transformer. Tesla headed back down the street and was surprised to see the car with the two men still sitting at the curb a hundred yards down the block. A smile crossed her face as she formed a plan. She pulled out her cell phone and punched in the numbers for an imaginary call. She faked the sort of argument two teenage lovers might have with more than average exasperation on her end.

"Don't you dare hang up on me," she said as he passed the car. "I'm not finished."

She pretended to redial the number while actually switching to camera mode and pressing the center button to take a picture. It was shadowy inside the FBI car, but she was pretty sure she could enhance the image on Barnaby's replacement computer with its state-of-the-art photo software. With the picture taken, she resumed her pantomime.

"That's your story? Oh, pull-eez."

"Ah, teenage love," Urbanski said after Tesla had gone safely past them and it was safe to talk.

Zoot didn't respond. The word "teenage" had sent him off on a different mental riff.

"So we done?" Urbanski finally said after a period of silence.

The question brought Zoot back to the moment.

"For tonight, yeah."

"Plummy back with you tomorrow?"

"No, you're stuck with me for a while. She's not feeling well. I told her to take a few days off."

What Zoot had actually told Plummy the morning after his visit was that he was concerned she might have a drinking problem and should take some time off to figure out if she did. If there was a problem, she should get some help — AA or something. He was not angry as Foster had been with him about his porno addiction. He sounded supportive. The bureau would be very understanding, he assured her.

"We have a number of people in rehab," he told her. "Given the pressures of what we do, it's not so surprising."

Aside from not wanting to have a partner who was a drunk, Zoot figured his advice, which he'd recorded in her personnel file, would give him grounds to argue that Plummy was making things up if she somehow guessed why her camera memory card was missing or had some boozy recollections about being undressed. He'd have the classic defense: she set me up.

* * *

After Tesla left, Barnaby set his alarm for 3 a.m. and was at the market by about 4:30, experiencing very little traffic on the way to the Bronx. The market had opened "late" that day at four and was already bustling with buyers from New York restaurants and owners of retail fish stores in the tri-state area. After his research on the market, he was not surprised to see that the majority were Asian, bidding on tuna for sushi or lesser offerings for fish balls. He told Victor to just go about his business, haggling privately over fish prices that were nowhere posted. He would just observe and take notes. By 9 a.m., the hectic day had died down and Victor signaled for Barnaby to follow him up the stairs to his office.

"So what'd you think?"

"Very old-fashioned. Like I said, no transparency on prices."

Victor smiled and said, "And as I said, that's exactly the way we want to keep it. I don't want to be selling at some price that's lower than some sucker will pay."

"I understand that perfectly, and it's great as long as you can get away with it, but someday someone will come along and offer real prices, and you may have to deal with it. That's what happened to the bond market."

"More likely I'd just deal with whoever tries that."

"OK. Just pointing the danger out, but if that is the way it is to be, do you understand what your buyers are saying about what they will pay? I noticed that many of them speak in a foreign language — Chinese or Japanese or something like that. I'm no linguist myself, but if you had someone who was fluent, it might be like listening on a confidential conversation without the buyers knowing."

"Huh," Victor said. "Hadn't thought of that. Smart."

"But don't get someone who looks Asian or they might be suspicious. Lots of kids learn Japanese or Mandarin in college, and with unemployment what it is, you might have your pick."

"What else?"

"I noticed some of the fish were fresher than others. Based on the clarity of their eyes."

Victor pursed his lips.

"I'm impressed. Not everyone knows that. Especially not a lot of the customers of these buyers."

"Well, if the customers are that ignorant, why not just freeze the fish you don't sell on Day One?"

"We don't sell frozen. This is the Fulton Fish Market or whatever it is we're calling it these days."

"As long as these buyers are tricking their customers, why not just give them another, healthier version of second-best? And that way, you wouldn't have to toss out fish on Day 3 the way I saw your workers doing this morning."

"I don't know. We never did it that way."

"Well, with the plan I've worked out for the stalls and the trucks, you'd have extra space and you could put in some freezers — which you could also use to make your own ice, so you don't have to buy that."

"Ice, huh? Yeah, maybe. And that would explain the freezers. I wouldn't have to bring attention to the frozen fish."

"Which you could just sell to supermarkets. Most of the ones I've seen sell mostly defrosted fish, and their customers don't seem to care."

"Seen that, too. A disgrace, but then most folks don't know how to cook fish, which is why they think Red Lobster is fine dining."

Barnaby laid out a series of other side businesses Victor could get into, creating a horizontal market in wholesale lemons, fish rubs, tartar sauces and other items fish buyers might want. Barnaby launched into his thoughts on how to streamline delivery of the fish when Victor cut him short.

"Can't do anything about the trucks. That's a touchy subject."

"You mean organized crime?"

Victor gave Barnaby a long look and then asked: "What you know about that?"

"I did a little research. The Giuliani days and the competitive bidding reforms. Seems to have cleaned things up a bit."

Victor cleared his throat and said, "Yeah, much better now. That whole mob thing was giving us guys with some Italian heritage a bad name, if you know what I mean."

"I can imagine, but now you have all the conditions for a vibrant modern business. A level playing field. What more could one ask?"

"Yeah. Sounds peachy."

Barnaby said he'd also noted in his informal checking of the scales that they were slightly off — in Victor's favor.

"Hmm. I'll have to check into that."

Barnaby told Victor he'd type up a plan for efficiency and new businesses and give it to him in a couple of days.

"On the house," as I promised but if you like the ideas, maybe I could help you with some of your other business."

Victor added: "Tell you what. I got a little garment factory in the city. Why don't you come over and take a look at that?"

Victor wrote down the address and told Barnaby to drop by the next day. Barnaby started to leave, but Victor told him to hold on a minute. He asked Crunch to get a package out of the top drawer of his filing cabinet. Crunch came back with something wrapped in a dish towel. Victor handed it to Barnaby.

"Next time those Chinese guys come back, this may help."

Barnaby took the item, which felt heavy, as if something metal were inside.

After he left, Crunch asked Victor, "What'd you give him that for? Might come back to bite you."

"Nah. Can't be traced to me. But I'm curious to see if he does anything with it. I want to know what kind of guy we're dealing with here. I've been playing him along on the time and motion B.S., partly because it's been free. But, turns out, he might save us some dough, and, more important, I think I can use a guy like this. We need to be getting out of the crook business and putting our dough into legit stuff. This guy knows legit. And he's legit. Nice front man. And he's so earnest — or at least seems so.

That's worth something. But if he's a little bent, that's good to know because I can always use an edge."

After Barnaby got back to his car, he opened the dish towel and discovered a small caliber handgun with the handle wrapped in medical tape. A small plastic bag next to it contained a supply of bullets. His instant reaction was to take it back to Victor, but he feared that might ruin his budding business relationship. He was sure Victor was just trying to be helpful. Barnaby decided he'd take the gun home and get rid of it as soon as he could. And not tell Victor.

Barnaby backed out of his parking space to begin his trip home. Special Agent Urbanski started up his engine to follow him but Zoot told him to stay put.

"I see someone else we know. Let's see what he's up to. We can always catch Mr. Gilbert at home."

What Zoot had seen was yet another Asian-looking man who'd arrived in a pickup truck with the name of a Chinatown restaurant painted on its doors. The man walked toward Victor's warehouse. What Zoot and Urbanski couldn't hear was the conversation that took place in Victor's office after the door was closed.

"Lin will come by your office in the city for a pickup and drop off," the Asian man said to Victor.

"Same designers as last season?"

"A few new ones. I don't have them all or I would have brought them with me."

Victor smiled.

"This is so old school. Burglary, I mean."

"My superiors like the concept. Everyone is expecting us to hack into the designers' computers. This way, we leave no fingerprints. No traceable algorithms or messages written on Chinese keyboards. The Americans have been getting a little too good at tracing things back to the mainland. We decided to try a little cooling-off period. Let them blame someone else for a while."

"Like mobsters, you mean?"

"Exactly."

"But they'll see you're still selling the goods."

"Easy to explain. This stuff is all over the Internet." The Asian man smiled. "It gives entrepreneurs ideas."

After the Asian man left the market, Urbanski, dressed in white coveralls in the surveillance van, took his picture.

"Except for the bad clothes, sure does look like First Secretary Wong again."

"He looked much nattier in his suit in Central Park when he shared that park bench with John Lin."

"So what do you think his deal is with Victor?"

"Haven't figured that one out yet, but they seem to have one interesting connection."

"Barnaby Gilbert?"

"Bingo."

"That makes as much sense as some caper that involves wholesale fish and counterfeit goods."

"Maybe we can get Mr. Gilbert to explain it all. We're gonna be all over him the next couple of days. And if he doesn't show us what he and all his pals are up to, maybe we can get someone over in the U.S. Attorney's Office to work up criminal charges. Cost Gilbert some defense-lawyer money."

Chapter 9

Victor's factory was off Seventh Avenue, not quite in the historic garment district but close enough to be a useful location. The card Victor had given Barnaby said "Cutting-Edge Designs," and that sort of gave a hint about how up-to-date the company's fashions were. Often they were on the street faster than the designers whose creations had been stolen by Victor's associates.

The main manufacturing floor was on two, which gave workers, not all of whom had official papers, a chance to head for the stairs or the fire escape instead of the elevators, which might contain pesky law enforcement agents. The key product the workers were making that week was a slinky knit dress that looked like a creation of a hot New York designer, who had the misfortune of easy-to-pick locks. The total look included a raw silk scarf in colors that softened or contrasted the dress fabric, depending on the hue. The scarf makers were at tables all along the windows, which were smudged with decades of dust and sweat, providing no real picture for snoopers of what was going on inside.

Barnaby had visited similar factories in his work for Montgomery & Co. and saw immediately some inefficiencies that could be corrected. He showed the foreman the card from Victor, which had a handwritten note on the back authorizing the visit. Barnaby took notes for about two hours before Victor arrived with Angelo in tow. Barnaby gave Victor a provisional run-down on how the tables and fabric supplies might be re-arranged. He gave his views on which part of the manufacturing process should go first, as well as how Victor might get more clothes out of the same amount of fabric.

Victor took that in, and, jerking his thumb to Barnaby, he told Angelo: "Genius." He added after a moment, "I might even pay him," laughing at his own joke. Barnaby, not sure what to say, just smiled.

Barnaby promised to write up his notes and make formal rec-ommendations.

"This one was a bit easy," he said. "I did a factory like this once for Calvin Klein."

"I did some Calvin Klein myself once," Victor said, winking at the foreman, whose name was Jerzy.

Barnaby said one key piece of information he needed was where the clothes would be sold so he could advise on delivery and related operations.

"Nothing complicated there," Victor said. "We got some places down on Canal Street. Very popular with the tourists."

"Ah. I know the area. You can get some very nice deals on purses, especially if you go into some rooms in the back. Not the real thing, of course, but they look genuine."

Victor looked at Barnaby for a moment, then said, "You get around, Barnaby. If I didn't know better I might think you were a cop."

"Me? Oh, no. That's much too dangerous. I'm a bird watcher on the weekends, you know. That's about my level of excite-ment."

Barnaby asked if Victor wanted any other businesses exam-ined. Victor said he had an Internet operation elsewhere in the building.

"But I think we should save that for another day," he said. "When I get to know you better."

"Of course."

"And if we get that far, you need to know, I demand total loyalty from people who work for me."

"Customer service is the cornerstone of any good business."

Victor put Barnaby's head in a friendly but firm hammerlock and said in a whisper, "That's a good attitude, Barnaby. You do what you're told, and you'll go far with me."

Barnaby, still smarting from the head kick from the Chinese intruder, finally let out a small cry of pain from the arm hold. Victor let Barnaby go and said: "Sorry, pal. Forgot about those Chinese guy. You want an Aleve or something?"

Barnaby shook his aching head.

"It's getting better. My only concern is they might come back."

"Hear ya. Those Chinese are tough. I deal with 'em all the time.

Victor winked. "But now you got a little edge."

Barnaby looked confused, then realized what Victor was talking about.

"Ah, yes. The package. Very kind of you."

After Barnaby left the factory, Jerzy asked Victor if he was really going to let Barnaby see the computer operation.

"Not right away. I got a couple of little tests for him first, and if he passes, then he could be really useful." Victor tapped his right temple with his index finger. "I got a plan for him."

"And if he doesn't pass?"

"Then he might need that gun I gave him."

* * *

Out on the street, Barnaby headed toward Grand Central, wondering if he'd see any of his regulars on the way home. He wasn't sure what he'd do if he saw one. He was reconsidering the wisdom his new hobby. He'd had some initial bad luck, but he decided, as he got to the terminal, that he wasn't going to give up quite yet.

Zoot and Special Agent Urbanski had fallen in behind him as he headed for 42d Street and were within pouncing range when they saw him cross the great hall on the way to Track 33.

"We should just arrest his ass and sweat him right now, Zoot," Urbanski said.

"Let's do it when he gets home, so there's less of a fuss. We don't want some public confrontation in the middle of Grand Central."

Barnaby didn't see anyone of interest on the train, which was an earlier one than he'd ever taken home from Montgomery & Co. At Yonkers, after enjoying the river view for a while, he pulled out the laptop Tesla had gotten from her friend. He liked the light weight and quick boot-up time. The fact that it could be used as a Mac or a PC, thanks to its dual-core chip, made Barnaby think about buying one of his own when the experiment was over. Clients might have either kind of files, so he'd be ready no matter what. It seemed the smart move.

Zoot and Urbanski, who'd sat in different seats on the way out of the city, joined up after they got off the train at Barnaby's stop and started to walk toward him. Before they got out of the parking lot, a deep male voice from behind said, "Mr. Ames, this would not be a good time to 'sweat' poor Mr. Gilbert, if that is what you had in mind."

Zoot pivoted and was confronted by a tall, lean black man with a shaved head and round, red glasses. He had a radio earpiece in his left ear. He wore gleaming black snakeskin cowboy boots under a gray, nailhead suit. He had a matching leather ID case, which he deftly flipped open to show his name was Vernon Waters and that he worked for another federal agency.

"NSA?" Zoot said. "What the hell do you guys want with Gilbert?"

"Let's say he's helping us out."

"He works for you?"

"In a manner of speaking."

"You know he's doing business with mobsters?" Urbanski asked.

The NSA man smiled and said, "He does seem to get around, but organized crime isn't our focus. We leave that up to the bureau."

"So what is your focus?" Zoot asked.

The man smiled.

"Not organized crime."

"Look, if you're not going to help us, why should we help you?"

"Let's say I might be able to provide you with some details from our investigations – as long as you don't let anyone know where you got it."

Zoot considered the offer.

"We'll think about it."

"Don't think too long. We have a lot of things of interest in our possession, including data on both of you."

"Got nothing to hide," Urbanski said.

Zoot wished he could say the same, but he just said, "We'll give you a week and see how it goes."

Waters pulled a business card out of his ID case and handed it to Zoot. It just had his name and a phone number on it.

"Keep in touch," Waters said.

Waters spoke softly into the sleeve of his suit jacket. A moment later, a late model Lexus pulled up with a beautiful, red-haired woman behind the wheel. The man got in on the passenger side, and the car took off.

"I don't like that guy," Urbanski said.

"I imagine a lot of people don't like that guy."

"Well if he doesn't give us anything we can use, Barnaby Gilbert is going to get that visit from us." Urbanski paused a moment then said, "How do you think he heard us talking about sweating him?"

"How to you think? He works for the NSA."

* * *

That was true, but what Zoot and Urbanski didn't know was that the confrontation with the NSA man had actually been triggered by Tesla, who'd sent her cell-phone photo of Zoot and Urbanski to her friend Veronica, who'd asked her former employer for a favor. As the Lexus headed south on 9A toward the city, Veronica said: "I owe you one, Vernon."

"Two actually. It took some doing to figure out who Ames was from that photo your little friend passed on to you.'

"Appreciate it."

"I still don't get why you want to go through all this for this Barnaby guy. What's he to you?"

"Nothing. It's my so-called little friend. The one I want you to hire. She's very fond of him. And I don't want her hurt if he gets into trouble."

"So is this professional or personal?"

"Yes," Veronica said.

* * *

Mr. Bo and Mr. Xi were sitting in their tinted-window van and had watched Barnaby arrive, followed by Zoot and Urbanski, the man they'd seen on Barnaby's street. Then came Waters and Veronica.

"More bad timing, it appears," Bo said.

"Either Gilbert is a federal agent and lied to us or he's in as much trouble with the U.S. government as he is with us."

"We should talk to John first. This has gotten more complicated."

Chapter 10

There had been talk about turning the original 1825 cell-block of Sing Sing into a tourist attraction, much like Alcatraz, but on that Saturday, the visiting hours at the prison were the normal ones — families only — and Dora was on time to talk with her dad. The date was an odd day of the month, which corresponded to the odd digit that ended her father's inmate number. Relatives of prisoners with even numbers at the end of their prison ID would be visiting on Sunday, according the rules set up by the prison, whose name was derived from a Native American phrase that meant "stone on stone."

That was fitting because the original prison had been built stone by stone by inmates from New York's Auburn unit, the second-oldest prison in the state. The Metro North commuter line that Barnaby had taken to Montgomery & Co. for years ran right through the prison with the older buildings located to the west of the tracks. Despite the concertina barb wire that adorned the walls of the railroad right-of-way, Dora felt a strange comfort as she made her weekday trips to the city and back, treating them like a quick visit home, given her father's proximity to the train she was on.

The prison had a storied history. It was the execution site of the Rosenberg spies and the setting of many Hollywood movies, including Jimmy Cagney's "Angels with Dirty Faces." It would make a nice tourist site, but other forces were pressing to tear the whole place down and make some money from condos and town houses, given the prison's million-dollar views of the Hudson.

Dora, who dealt with the short-term reality that Sing Sing would remain a prison as various forces fought over its future, arrived about nine that morning, knowing it would take till about 10:30 a.m. for her father to be called and transferred to the large visitors room. She brought plenty of change and singles so she and her dad could take advantage of the many vending machines the room offered. Big families got tables for the visit. Dora and her father had to sit side by side on chairs – one of the many rules.

Another was a ban on sexy clothing. No bare midriffs or backs or see-through tops. No tank tops or short shorts. Dora pushed the strictures a bit, wearing tight jeans and a red T-shirt that left little to the imagination. She had tossed on a black hoodie to cover it up, and the guard let her through.

Only after she had entered the room did she take it off to reveal the custom lettering she'd had made up at a T-shirt store near Times Square. It said "Truth will set you free. Lock picks too."

Her dad laughed when he saw it.

"Good one. I could use a pick on my bad days. Even without them, I think I could break out of this place."

"Don't even think about that. You're at the end. Assuming good behavior, of course."

"Don't worry. I keep adding up the money we've been making while I was in here. It will be worth the wait."

"Business is pretty good, including my little part."

"Careful. This is not a secure room. Officially I'm just a wrongly convicted dad, and you're just a poor little student. That's the parole-board story."

"Ex-student. Now a low-wage worker, who occasionally meets with that new friend of yours. From Connecticut. He's seems happy by the way."

"You still meeting at the same place?"

"Yeah. One new thing: instead of just taking what we find, he's starting to ask if we can look into certain things. If you know what I mean."

"Yeah. That's good. Maybe we can make a little more."

"He even gave me a bonus the last time. Nice Cartier watch."

Dora pulled up her left sleeve and showed her dad what appeared to be the famous Santos model.

Her father laughed.

"I'd have that checked out. That guy is cheap. Could be a knockoff."

"I think he's just trying to get in my pants."

Her father's eyes narrowed.

"Maybe you should stop wearing such provocative clothes."

Dora shrugged.

"It's what kids wear, though I do have to deal with the occasional perv."

Her father moved his face closer to hers.

"Like who?"

She shrugged.

"No one in particular. Besides, I got my knife. I can take care of myself."

Her father laughed.

"Sometimes you scare me."

"Good. When you're gone, maybe I'll run things."

Dora's dad laughed.

"Sure. You got enough money?"

"For my parole-board role as the poor prisoner's daughter, yeah. But I'd be happier with a share of the profits." Dora smiled sweetly. "Or a town car to take me to the city. But I'm doing OK...I got a little sideline to bring in a few dollars."

"I probably don't want to know."

Dora shrugged.

"Nothing really dangerous."

"All right, but if any creeps bother you, like that kid at the high school, you tell me."

"For a gangster, you're such a worrier."

* * *

John Lin had had to make an unexpected trip back to Shanghai and so was unavailable that weekend to talk securely to Bo and Xi about what to do about Barnaby. Thus Barnaby was able to spend a good part of his weekend blissfully birding at the point and up at Georges Island, a few miles north of his house. He and some fellow birders, who had picked him up at his house, were looking for the first eagles of the season. But it had been a warm autumn, and as the calendar pushed toward Thanksgiving, all they managed to see were hawks and some turkey vultures.

Barnaby heard an owl at the point but didn't see one at the usual site near the upper visitor's parking lot. He spotted a kestrel sitting on a light tower of the Croton-Harmon train station on his way back from the Croton River, where he'd recorded some sightings in his bird journal under his listings for cygnus olor, branta Canadensis and pandion haliaetus — swans, Canada geese and an osprey.

On Sunday, Tesla came over to watch the Jets game on Barnaby's HDTV, which, if Barnaby were honest, he'd bought more for her than himself. He watched Animal Planet sometimes, but more often than not he just read something or delved into his vinyl collection to listen to Gilbert and Sullivan or some Broadway show. Sometimes, when alone, he sang along to the memorized lyrics, channeling a modern major general or the Music Man.

Tesla made some microwave popcorn, most of which they ate during the first quarter. During the commercial break she asked how Barnaby's loaner computer was working out. Barnaby mentioned his thought about buying one like it.

"How is your friend doing with my old computer?" he asked.

"Hasn't said. Takes a while to monitor these things. She did say one strange thing, though."

"What's that?"

"If some government official asks about your computers or what's on them, just say you've been told not to talk about that."

"Should I mention her?"

"God, no. Just be vague. She said that should work."

Chapter 11

On Monday, Dora took her normal train — Barnaby's usual train — to the city, but Barnaby was not aboard. He was working at home on his borrowed computer on a report for Victor's garment operation. Dora stared down the come-hither looks of the one boys of her age who summoned up enough courage to try to snag her attention. Shot down, he retreated to the safety of his music player and looked out the window as if the river were the most important thing on his mind.

She walked to Madam's Selma's, her light blue wool skirt swiveling back and forth as she sashayed south, ear buds in place, listening to John Lee Hooker sing "Good Morning, Little School Girl." She earned more than a few looks from male admirers and was pleased that her little pantomime had had the reaction it had. The skirt was part of a school uniform she sometimes wore when she wanted to drive some stupid man wild with that ridiculous sex fantasy. The Japanese paid a ton just to have her sit on their laps and do a gentle grind. She found them amusing but kept her gravity knife handy just in case. Money was power, she had found, but sex was so much more.

Clarence Foster, Zoot's former boss, was in the surveillance van when Dora arrived. The whorehouse was an organized crime asset, which gave him jurisdiction. The financial crime supposedly being committed inside was a new wrinkle in an ongoing investigation. Foster and Special agent Mike Rooney had watched Dora take her time mounting the stone steps, laboring as if she were heading to chemistry class or something else she considered a bore.

"That's Dmytro Pivo's kid," Rooney told Foster, who was sitting in on the stakeout for the day.

"What's with the uniform? She's not in school, is she?"

"Not that we can tell. At least not in the school that uses that uniform. And, as we know, that's no school house."

"So what's she up to?"

"Haven't put any bugs in there to find out. No probable cause yet. All we know is that our hedge fund buddy comes here couple times a month. Pivo's kid is here on the exact same days, so it makes us wonder."

"We don't have to wonder about the profits his fund is making, and our tipster says it's because of insider info. Maybe some of Pivo's goons got a hot tip hacking into somebody's network."

"Pivo's guys certainly have access to a lot of stuff. Deals and such."

"Not Pivo himself, though."

"No. He gets no access to computers in the slammer."

"But he does get access to his daughter."

"Right. She could be the go-between to sell info to hedge-fund boy."

"But our pals at the SEC say nothing's being done in hedge guy's name. Somebody in his firm makes the trade or they make a bundle for some customer, who trades right after they issue some research saying something is a good buy."

"So then it looks like they were just following smart analysis."

"Exactly, so we need to catch our guy getting the info in the first place."

"Sounds like we're going to have to put a bug in there."

"Hard to do. Even if we get probable cause, Madam Selma never closes, so the bug planter would have to be a customer."

"Happy to volunteer."

"No way. You look too much like an FBI agent. It'd take someone less suspicious. Somebody who looks harmless."

*   *   *

Barnaby finished his report for Victor by lunchtime, made himself a tuna salad sandwich and had a glass of skim milk before he caught an afternoon train to the city. The train was eerily empty at that time of day. There were a few sleeping commuters, mostly Hispanic. Barnaby guessed they were headed for a job that started late and ended late. He saw none of his regulars. With no one to wonder about, he enjoyed the view of the river and the Palisades, which looked dark maroon at that time of day rather than the burnished gold he was used to in the morning when the rising sun focused its trillion-watt klieg light on the stone and grass surface that an intractable glacier had carved out ages before.

Victor wasn't at the factory, so Barnaby went over his suggestion for changes with his foreman, the only non-Hispanic amid a sea of faces that would have been more appropriate for an immigration-processing center. Barnaby took about an hour with Jerzy. He was on his way out of the building when his eye noticed the directory and he spotted the name of a tech company on the eighth floor. Victor had mentioned he had a computer operation elsewhere in the building and that he might have him take a look at it too. Glancing at his watch, Barnaby saw it was only 4:30 and decided he might pop into the tech company's office to give it a preliminary scan for any work Victor might want done. If he saw some inefficiencies, he might even get a job he otherwise wouldn't. One thing he had learned at Montgomery

& Co.: success in business often came to those who took the initiative.

Barnaby got off on eight and found a hallway with many plain wooden and frosted glass doors that gave no hint about who or what might be behind them. He walked to the end of the hall before he found one with the name of the company, Internet Services Inc. The door had multiple locks, a peephole and a video camera above the jamb. He pressed the buzzer. Nothing happened for about a minute. Barnaby was about to press it again when a trim young man with a couple of days worth of beard opened it a crack and asked in a slight Slavic accent what Barnaby wanted. Barnaby explained his relationship to Victor, whose name caused the man to open the door a bit wider. That allowed Barnaby to see rows of men and women sitting in front of various models of slim laptops.

"So what kind of business is this?" Barnaby asked.

The young man, still not inviting Barnaby in, waited a moment before saying: "Sort of a call center."

"Ah, giving those folks in Bangalore a run for their money, huh?"

The man looked puzzled at first, then answered: "Something like that."

"Why laptops, though? You could get a better price on networked desktops."

The man's eyes narrowed at the question.

"Makes it easier to get out of here in a hurry."

"I'm sorry?"

The man paused, then said: "Like for a fire."

"Ah, good thinking. Then you don't lose your equipment or data. And people can work at home if needed. A smart move."

The man just nodded. Barnaby asked if he could come in and look around. The man, who didn't introduce himself, said he'd have to clear it with Victor. Barnaby said he understood and left, wondering why a call center had so few people on the phone and so many fixated on their computer screens. Surely there must be some inefficiency there.

After he left, the man phoned Victor and filled him in. Victor was surprised at the unauthorized visit, but wrote it off to the eager-beaver attitude that seemed part of Barnaby's makeup. Still, he told his computer operations chief not to let Barnaby in if he came back.

"You think he's a cop?"

"My gut tells me no, so for now I'm going to cut him some slack 'cause I got plans for him. But we'll watch him a little more closely. One of my guys is going to break into his house, and we'll see what we see."

Victor took the opportunity to get an update on his computer operation.

'Think we scored big today. Found a stupid bank. Big money-center one."

"How's that?"

"These idiots use customer account numbers and IDs in the Internet address they assign you once you log into you account online."

"How'd you figure that out?"

"One of our hackers opened a free checking account and noticed it, so now were doing variations on his number to see what other accounts we can get into. We've wired about three hundred grand to our mules down in Texas. End of the week, it'll be in one of our Eastern European accounts."

*　*　*

Barnaby walked to Grand Central after his visit to Internet Services Inc. He was pleasantly surprised to see he could catch his regular train home. He found a window seat in his usual car and enjoyed the sinful pleasure of a Daily News on the way north, catching up on the latest scandals, murders and weird stories about New Yorkers that made his own life seem so much more normal and safe.

There were no reports of headless torsos in topless bars or stories about members of Congress posting pictures of their engorged penises, but some rabbis in Brooklyn had been arrested by the FBI the day before on charges of money laundering. One of them was accused of selling human organs on the black market. Despite the publicity about Bernard Madoff and his $65 billion Ponzi scheme, similar con games seemed to pop up every month. One in the paper that day involved a lawyer who said he'd spotted a previously unnoticed gap in dollar-euro trading that offered a can't-lose return to the lucky clients who signed up with him. He'd netted a mere $25 million. Most of his victims were senior citizens who'd been looking to increase their meager retirement income in some way surer than putting everything on black.

When the train stopped at 125th Street, Barnaby spotted Dora getting on, dressed in her blue uniform. She saw him too and shot him an icy look as she took a seat on the other side of the aisle. Barnaby found himself feeling a little embarrassed after his earlier encounter with her, and he read more of the Daily News than he otherwise might have so as not to make eye contact with her during the ride.

When the train pulled into Barnaby's stop about 45 minutes later, Dora headed for the exit nearest her seat. Barnaby chose the one at the other end of the car even though it was farther from his seat than the one Dora had picked. It permitted him to exit the station sooner than Dora, and he picked up his pace on his walk home so as not to have another confrontation. About half a block from the station he felt a fist punch him in the lower back, and a pain shot through his body, stopping him in his tracks.

"I told you not to follow me, you creep!" Dora said.

Barnaby caught his breath and explained: "I wasn't following you. I was ahead of you."

That stopped Dora for a moment before she said, "Don't get cute...and stay off my train from now on."

"It's my train too. I was just going home."

Dora considered that.

"So where do you live in case I want to have someone punch your lights out?"

Barnaby hesitated to give his address in case physical punishment was what Dora really had in mind. He tried a vaguer response.

"I live on the same street as a friend of yours. Tesla. Tesla Finch."

"No friend of mine. And I think she may be playing for the other team, if you know what I mean."

Barnaby didn't know what that meant, so he just added: "Well, she's a very nice young lady and smart and talented."

"What's with you and young girls? You got something going with her?"

"The only thing we have going is that she helps me with my computer, and she's a fellow train hobbyist."

"Plays with your trains, huh? You steam into her tunnel or something?"

"It's nothing like that."

"Yeah, I'm sure. But if you want play trains with me, it's gonna cost you. Couple of hundred at least. So next time, just show me the money."

*　*　*

Special Agent Rooney snapped Barnaby's encounter with Dora through a telephoto lens. He and Foster had followed her on the train from Madam Selma's after having a third agent follow the hedge-fund manager.

"Isn't that the dork we saw over at Madame Selma's?"

"I think you're right. Wonder what he's doing up here."

* * *

After Barnaby got home, he got a call from Angelo who wondered if they could meet that night to discuss some business options for his new consulting service. Angelo said he was in the area and suggested a pizzeria on Main Street.

"Just finished with another client. If that's convenient. My treat."

Barnaby knew that eventually the pizza would be his treat by the time Angelo sent his first bill. And he had a slow-cooker meal ready to eat. But he decided to take Angelo up on the offer, partly because he'd gotten some free advice to that point and because he could save the beef stew for the next day.

Angelo went over some of the home-office options and provided a list of expenses that might be deducted. Barnaby knew enough tax law so that a lot of it wasn't a revelation, but he found it reassuring that a professional was giving his stamp of approval to some things Barnaby had thought might be valid for tax purposes.

Angelo didn't seem in a hurry and talked about how challenging it was to have teenage daughters and how the Mets had driven him crazy again with a string of losses. He asked Barnaby about his late wife and how much he had left on his mortgage and what kind of life insurance he had. By the time they were done, an hour had passed.

That was enough time for two of Victor's knuckle-draggers, Crunch and Geek, to break into Barnaby's place. It wasn't hard. The locks were pretty primitive. Geek, who got his nickname because of his criminal capabilities with computers, copied the hard drive of Barnaby's loaner computer. Crunch searched drawers and a lone file cabinet for anything of interest. They were done in 45 minutes. Not having received a call from Angelo to signal the end of his meeting with Barnaby, they walked calmly out the back door and made their way to their car on the next block without attracting any attention.

"Good news and bad news," Geek said when he called Victor.

"Bad news first."

"Couldn't crack some of the files on his computer. Encrypted up the ying-yang, and looks like he's signed up for that cloud thing I told you about, so not much stored on his hard drive. We can get the guys on the eighth floor to see about those coded files, and if we need to, we can come back and ask him some questions — personally."

"And the good news?"

"Nothing hinky in the house unless you count snakes and bunch of reptiles and a big train set down in the basement. This guy is one weird dude."

"But no sign he's a cop?"

"No. But I still think that's a question. We just need to figure out how to answer it."

"I got an idea."

Chapter 12

The next day, Zoot noticed Rooney's train-station photos in the morning routings Foster had sent around. He looked at the snapshots of Barnaby with Dora, who was identified as the daughter of a convicted Ukrainian computer fraudster. They confused Zoot more than ever. What the heck was Barnaby? Zoot didn't buy that Barnaby was some NSA operative, despite what the guy in the snakeskin cowboy boots had said. He was probably something between a stone crook and a moron way over his head. Whatever Barnaby was, Zoot had decided Barnaby could be useful to get the bureau inside some criminal operations. He'd find a way to put Barnaby to work as a confidential informant, willing or unwilling.

His preference was that Barnaby was a crook because that would make him more intelligent than he seemed, and threat of prosecution and an offer of immunity would give him the incentive to cooperate. Zoot knew he didn't have a lot of proof that Barnaby had broken any laws, but conspiracy charges were easy to make, and he'd use that dodge if Barnaby resisted.

Whether Barnaby played the fool or actually was one, Zoot really didn't care. If a fool, he'd make him a Junior G Man, and if things went sour, hey, it happens. Collateral damage. Zoot needed a break to get his career back on track. Means to an end, he told himself, battling to concentrate on his cases as pesky images of Dora flitted across his mind's eye. And fuck that guy at the NSA. Maybe they knew about his nasty little habit, maybe they didn't. He'd be careful connecting with Barnaby. A conversation away from listening ears was what he had in mind. Nothing on the phone or indoors.

*   *   *

Barnaby was working at home that morning and heard the doorbell ring about 11. Zoot was alone and showed Barnaby his FBI credentials. He said he had a matter of grave importance to discuss and wondered if Barnaby could take a little ride. Barnaby had the feeling he'd seen Zoot somewhere in the previous few days but couldn't quite place him. On the train maybe? He got his jacket and rode with Zoot north. They made small talk about the weather and sports, till Barnaby spotted the turnoff for the point.

"That's a good spot for a conversation — unless you want to stay in the car," Barnaby said, trying to be helpful. "Not many people around this time of day. The birders and gone, so just down to some late dog walkers. Retirees mostly."

"You seem to know it pretty well."

"I'm a birder. Come here all the time."

Zoot flashed a thin smile.

"When your not in the Garment District or Hunts Point."

Barnaby's eyes blinked at Zoot's knowledge of his recent whereabouts.

"That's right," Barnaby finally said, deciding not to ask too many questions. "It's one of the best spots in the county."

"Really?"

"Oh, yes, I've filled up my life book considerably just from what I spotted or heard right in this park. It's the garbage dump, if you ask me."

"The garbage dump?"

"See that hill on the left?" Barnaby said as Zoot's car neared the park entrance. "Well, that's a landfill, and the gulls and eagles and bigger birds like what runs around on top of it. Mice and such."

"Eagles?"

"Yes, Bald Eagles."

"I thought they were extinct."

"Oh, no. They've come way back since the river got cleaned up. They're out here for breakfast or dinner in the winter. Any day now, we'll be seeing them soaring overhead looking for ducks or fish to snatch."

"Fascinating," Zoot said without enthusiasm as he pulled his car into a lot at the far end of the point.

"It really is. I can give you a little tour of the best spots while we talk. I was out here recently. I arrived a bit late, but I still saw an American Black Duck, a Bufflehead Duck, a Black-Capped Chickadee, a Brown Creeper, a Belted Kingfisher and a Red-Bellied Woodpecker. Got some nice shots. I only wish I'd brought my binoculars and camera today. I would have if I'd known we were coming here."

"Next time I'll call you in advance."

"Thanks. It might be worth your while. This Indian Summer is mixing up the birds a bit. We might see something really special if we're lucky."

"Swell." Zoot wasn't interested in birds at all and got to the point of his visit: "So you're good with a camera and binoculars?"

Barnaby smiled.

"I always get my bird."

"You might appreciate these, then," Zoot said as he handed over a series of photos that included John Lin, Victor Dragon and Dora Pivo, some with Barnaby in them, including a couple at Madam Selma's whore house, plus some with Lin with Mr. Wong, the Chinese consulate employee in Central Park.

He waited for any nervous or surprised reaction from Barnaby but got none.

"These are very good quality," Barnaby said. "500-mm lens?"

Zoot wasn't sure what to make of that, so he just answered, "Some 500, some 200."

"Birders need the 500 for the real close-up stuff but sometimes if I'm real quiet and I hold my breath, I can manage with a 200, which is much lighter. But you probably know that."

"I usually have others take the photos. I'm more interested in what they capture, and I find these a little puzzling."

"I guess you would if you don't see the connection"

"And what is the connection?"

"My train."

Zoot's forehead crinkled as he took that in.

"Your train?"

"Yes. Mr. Lin and Dora take my train, and I just followed them to see where they went."

"Why did you follow them?"

"Sort of a hobby. Like birding. Actually very much like birding. I write down what I see and take pictures. And often I get surprised, just like with the train people. You never know what to expect."

Zoot pondered that.

"Tell me about the surprises."

"Well, like the time I was following the hoots of an owl. A horned owl. And I ran smack into a coyote. I can tell you, that stopped me right in my tracks. You don't want to fool with a coyote."

Zoot let out an exasperated breath.

"I meant the surprises with the people you followed."

"Oh, sorry. Of course. Well, they're not as dangerous as coyotes. At least not so far, but they can get a little irritated sometimes."

Barnaby fingered the spot where the Chinese intruder had kicked him.

"What about Mr. Lin?"

"Um, he seems to be involved in selling counterfeit handbags and such. Not what I expected at all.

"And all these people you've run into were on your train?"

"Well, not all. Sometimes the people I followed led me to other people, who led me to other people. It's really quite fascinating. It may seem like some great big coincidence, but it's really not. It's a bit like chaos theory. You know. Ricochets."

"Chaos theory?"

"Yes like when a drop of rain on the East coast can lead to some gigantic storm in California. That sort of thing. Unintended consequences."

"Uh, huh. So where does Victor come in?"

"Unintended consequences. I followed Mr. Lin before I knew his name, and I met a man in a building where Mr. Lin stopped for something, and he introduced me to Angelo my accountant, who introduced me to Victor...You just never know, you know?"

"Not really. So what if I told you that Mr. Lin has a connection with Victor and Victor with Dora and her dad?"

"Well that's pretty improbable, even for chaos theory."

"That's what I was thinking."

Barnaby considered that and then said: "I noticed I'm in a lot of these photos. We're you following me?"

"Initially. You might say you became our hobby just as these people became yours. We didn't know what to think of you and so we just tagged along."

Barnaby chuckled.

"So you thought I might be some sort of criminal mastermind?"

"We didn't know what to think. Still don't. Might be a connection. Might not. If you help us, we'd be able to eliminate you and maybe some others as suspects."

"You mean I'd be like your deputy?"

"Sort of."

Barnaby nodded his head at the idea.

"OK. Anything to help law enforcement. I'm already part of our Neighborhood Watch, so I do semi-police work on the side."

Zoot managed a strained smile.

"Very impressive."

Zoot couldn't figure out if Barnaby was playing him, but he knew how he might figure that out. Zoot pulled out two electronic bugs from his jacket pocket and handed them to Barnaby.

"Know what those are?"

"Some sort of electronic component?"

"Listening devices. I'd like you to go somewhere and plant them."

"Plant them? You mean like an undercover job?"

Zoot nodded.

"Think you could do it?"

"I guess. Where would I have to go?"

"You know that house you visited when you followed Dora?"

"The one in Harlem?"

"That's the one. She works there sometimes, and some of the agents think she meets someone there, and we want to see what they say. All you have to do is go inside and plant the bugs.

Zoot could see Barnaby hesitating.

"That a problem?"

"Not if I bring a couple of hundred dollars."

Chapter 13

The next day, Barnaby got to the station at his regular time but stopped at a spot away from foot traffic. Through his binoculars, he saw Dora go up the stairs to the station. After her train pulled out, he took a later one. He wanted to avoid having Dora see him walking behind her on her way to Madam Selma's. He feared if she confronted him on the street, he'd never have the courage to get inside – and she might cut him with her knife. That was still a danger once he got inside, but he hoped the money Zoot had given him would be enough to prevent that.

He wasn't relishing the conversation with Dora once he gained entry, but he felt he was duty-bound to help the FBI and had a plan to deal with the problem. Not much of one, he had to admit, but at least it was something. He remembered that Dora had a regular appointment before noon with the man in a limousine he'd seen on his first visit to the house. With that in mind, he threaded the time needle and got to the house just before ten. Madame Selma answered the door. A sly smile broke over her face.

"Welcome back, grandpa. You finally figure out what you want?"

"I'd like to talk to Dora. And I brought the money."

Madame Selma's eyes narrowed.

"How'd you know her name?"

"We're sort of neighbors."

Selma harrumphed a bit.

"You sure you know what you're getting into? I've got a lot of nice girls who'd be a lot less dangerous than Dora."

"I'm sure. Dora is who I want."

"You know who her dad is?"

"I know he's in prison."

Selma let out a light laugh.

"That is the least of it, pal. You do anything rough or funny with her, and you are a dead man. Understand?"

"I don't plan anything funny — or rough. I just want to talk to her. She said to bring some money, and I have."

Barnaby took out five $100 bills from his jacket pocket and showed Selma, who was dressed that day in a black and gold embroidered Egyptian caftan. She had on silver eye makeup that made her look like she was about to sing the role of Aida.

"OK, but she has to agree first, so you stay put till I ask her."

Barnaby walked past the heavy wood and frosted glass door and stopped on the black and white tile foyer floor.

"JEW-LEE-ANN!" Selma shouted as he stopped. Moments later a heavily muscled bald man dressed in a tight red T-shirt and matching cotton pants trotted down the hallway. A dish towel flecked with flour was still in his left hand.

"If he moves before I get back, smash him."

Julian nodded and stood guard silently, arms crossed as he stared at Barnaby. Barnaby pursed his lips nervously as Selma mounted the carpeted steps. He counted the moments till her return, which seemed an eternity.

"She'll see you," Selma said after she got back. "Don't know why. But she seemed amused. It's the room at the top of the stairs. The Blue Room."

Barnaby went up the stairs carefully, producing creaks on most of the risers. The door at the top of the landing was ajar, the only one that wasn't closed. He pushed the door lightly with his right hand and entered cautiously.

"I fucking knew it," Dora said. "I knew what you were after from the get-go."

"Well, maybe not. I just want to talk to you."

"Right."

"Really."

"And you're willing to pay."

"Yes. You said that was the deal."

Barnaby brought out the $500 again, splaying the bills for Dora.

"You said a couple of hundred. I bought a little extra."

"Well, isn't that sweet."

Dora walked over to Barnaby and snatched all of the money. She went over to a window, pulled the curtains back and held the bills up to the sunlight. Satisfied, she put the money in the side pocket of her school uniform.

"So, some rules. Like I said, I only do a couple of things. Lap dance. Lotion massage. Hand job basically. A BJ, if I feel like it, which is rare, like if you are really hung. Other than that, no penetrations. Got it?"

Barnaby blinked at the frankness of her explanation.

"I think so."

"Good, so what's it going to be?"

"Could we just talk?"

"Yeah, but then what?"

"Nothing really. That will be enough."

Dora laughed.

"It's your money. But if we're going to talk, first I have to pee."

Dora walked to the bathroom door but stopped before she went into the room.

"You want to watch me?"

Barnaby boggled at the strange offer and said in a halting voice, "No thanks."

Dora laughed again, went in and closed the door. It took Barnaby a while to realize he had a golden opportunity to plant the bugs Zoot had given him. He went over to the queen-size bed in the room, got down on his knees and placed one of the eavesdropping devices in the springs under the mattress. Bug implanted, he stood up quickly in case Dora came out unexpectedly. A few moments later, Barnaby heard the toilet flush and when the sink faucet began running he slipped the other bug behind a reproduction of Eloise, the fictive resident of the Plaza Hotel, which hung over the bed. Dora finally came out dressed in a Japanese silk robe with large cranes printed on it. She had fuzzy pink mules on her feet.

"I figured I'd get comfortable if we're going to talk, she said, a wicked smile on her face.

"Sure," Barnaby said, sounding nervous.

"Have a seat."

Other than the bed, the only place to sit was a wooden chair in front of a matching desk, the plain type a high school student might have in her bedroom. Barnaby sat down and took stock of the room. The walls had college pennants from Ivy League schools, pom-poms on top of a blond wood dresser that matched the bed and desk. A small bookcase held a complete set of Nancy Drew novels. A vintage 45-rpm record player stood on a stand with a collection of music stored on a shelf underneath. A signed photo of Elvis was in the corner of the desk, which had papers, notebooks and other evidence of schoolwork on top.

"Do you sleep here?" Barnaby asked after his inspection.

Dora laughed again.

"No, silly. This is fantasy. We have an S&M room with chains and stuff. And one lady is a wet nurse. Sort of icky to me, but some guys love that. Momma's boys, I guess. And there's a dominatrix. You may know her. She's from the village, too."

"I don't think so."

"And I'm the virgin schoolgirl," Dora said, putting her right index finger to her chin as she struck a coy pose.

Barnaby looked puzzled, so Dora continued: "People pay to play out their fantasies."

"Doesn't your father mind?"

"Mind? He owns this place. I'm just here for on-the-job training. Well, to a point. I need to understand what the girls go through. So this month I'm the virgin school girl."

Not totally computing, Barnaby replied: "A virgin is a good model. Saving yourself for marriage, that is. That's what my wife and I did."

"Hellooooo, strange man. We call our planet Earth. What do you call yours?"

Barnaby considered the question seriously.

"I'm from earth too."

Dora let out a breath of exasperation.

"Look, numbnuts, Virgin, smirgin. I'm just here to learn the business and pick up some spending money. Sort of like a paid internship."

Barnaby nodded.

"Internships are often a good career move."

Dora gave Barnaby a long, tolerant look, then came over to his chair, turned around and sat on his lap. She leaned back and sniffed a couple of times.

"What's that you're wearing."

"I forget the name. Something lemony. I got it in the city. They said ladies like it."

"That's sweet. You put it on to impress me?"

"I, I'm not really sure. It's not what I use for work."

"Isn't that special. How about a little lap dance?"

Dora began a gentle grind. Barnaby, feeling the impact below his waist, cleared his throat and carefully pushed Dora off his lap.

"Not at the moment," he said, not wanting to offend.

"Really? So a hand job?"

"I just want to talk,"

"About what?"

Barnaby hadn't prepared for this part of his visit and didn't really have a topic. With Dora looking at him impatiently, he grasped for one and chose something he knew.

"You ever see the swans that swim along the Hudson near our station?"

Dora shook her head.

"I sit on the other side."

"You should switch sometime. They're quite magnificent and quite different from most birds."

"Like how?"

"Well, they live in pairs for life, and if one dies the other goes on alone. It's quite sad."

"So what's that got to do with me?"

"You remind me of a swan. You have a long beautiful neck."

Dora, staring down at Barnaby, lost the taunting look on her face, stood up and said, "This is boring. Just get out. And I'm keeping the money."

"Sure."

Barnaby stood up and headed for the door.

"Wait a minute," Dora said before he opened it.

Barnaby turned around.

"Selma said you had a camera last time you came. You got it with you?"

Barnaby didn't have his SLR with him, but he pulled out his point-and-shoot one. Dora struck a glamorous pose with her hands on her hips and told Barnaby to take her picture.

"So you get something for your money."

Barnaby snapped a shot using the automatic mode so he didn't have to think about the light setting. Using the LCD screen on the back of the camera to compose the image, he pressed the shutter button.

"One more," Dora said.

Barnaby raised the camera to his eye again. Dora began a 3-2-1 countdown. When she said "Go!" Barnaby snapped the photo without thinking and only realized after the fact that Dora had opened her robe and provided a full frontal view of her body.

"But, but why?" was all Barnaby could manage before turning in panic and rushing out the door and down the stairs. He walked down the block east toward FDR Drive. He passed a van with Agent Rooney in it and turned the corner. He saw Zoot in an unmarked sedan where he said he'd be. Barnaby looked over his shoulder to see if he'd been followed. He didn't see anyone and got in quickly.

"How'd it go?" Zoot asked.

"One under the bed and one behind a picture."

Zoot asked Special Agent Urbanski in the back seat if he was receiving any transmissions.

"Loud and clear. She's got some music on. Hip hop. And our hedge fund guy is due any minute from what the case file says, so we should have a front-row seat."

Zoot smiled at Barnaby.

"You did good."

Barnaby pulled out his camera and popped out the memory card that held the two photos of Dora.

"You might want these," he said. "I took two photos. She asked me to."

"She asked you?"

"Yes. I also recorded the session. Figured it might come in handy."

Barnaby reached into his inside jacket pocket and pulled out a digital recorder.

"I'd like the recorder back. You can keep the photos."

Zoot gave Barnaby a ride to the 125th Street Station and told him he'd be in touch.

"We may have anther assignment."

"Not with Dora, I hope," Barnaby said.

*   *   *

As Urbanski was monitoring the conversation inside Madame Selma's, another government agent was monitoring Urbanski.

"Why is a counterfeit-goods unit eavesdropping on what seems like an organized-crime case?" the agent monitoring Urbanski said. "Especially with an organized-crime unit right down the street."

"Not sure," said a second government agent, who was dressed in black snakeskin cowboy boots. "But I am glad we decided to make sure Special Agent Ames left Barnaby Gilbert alone."

"So now he's busted for disobeying orders?"

"Better than that," said Vernon Waters. "I'm betting he hasn't told anyone what he's doing in that house, including his office and a federal judge, so now we got two things on him."

*   *   *

Zoot headed back to the office, where he fired up his personal laptop. When it was ready, he inserted the memory card Barnaby had given him and plugged some earphones into Barnaby's recorder. Zoot clicked on his photo program and downloaded the shots of Dora. Zoot was pleased with the first one of her but became transfixed when he saw the second. Dora's modest breasts and shaved body seared an indelible image into his brain. As he was staring, Clarence Foster knocked on the jamb of Zoot's open office door. Zoot calmly clicked on the minus sign of the photo image, and Dora disappeared from the screen.

"What's up?" Foster asked.

"Just checking out a suspect."

Foster's brow furrowed.

"On your personal laptop?"

"Our CI took a photo, so I have to use my laptop for the SD card. We don't have a SD port on the desktop. We should, you know."

Foster didn't look completely satisfied with the answer as he nodded his head while contemplating it. In the end, all he said was, "Right." Then he left.

Zoot exhaled a long breath. He knew he'd dodged a bazooka round. He also felt smug that he'd injected himself into Foster's insider-trading case and that he'd have a plausible explanation for the trespass when he presented the breakthrough results of his bugging of Dora's room. Foster would owe him one. Maybe not enough to transfer him back to his old job, but it would be a start. And if he played his Barnaby card for a few more things, he might get all the way there.

He'd also survived to look at the pretty pictures of Dora another day. Or any day. Why wait, in fact, he asked himself. Foster was gone. The danger was past, Zoot told himself as he clicked on the photo card icon and brought up Dora's pictures again. He advanced to the second one and lingered. After a few moments, he got rid of the screen images and popped out the memory card, putting it in his right pants pocket.

He had his hands on the top of his laptop's screen as if about to close the unit, but instead he clicked on his browser. He took a deep breath and considered what he was about to do and the danger of doing it. On the search line he typed in "sexy school-girl" and hit the return key. Up came a variety of results. He clicked on a dozen in a row, most of them professional porn actors with tattoos. He found none so provocative as Dora.

Barnaby had taken the train home from 125th Street. It was a local, which he normally never liked. A waste of time, but it was the first one to arrive at the station, and, finding himself a bit disoriented after his visit with Dora, he climbed aboard and found that all the window seats on the river side were taken. He took one on the other side instead and found himself staring at rocks, weeds and railroad junk, an unwatchable view that put him into a dozing state.

He dreamed but not a semi-conscious daydream in which he controlled the story line. Nothing about spotting a rare bird or becoming a rich entrepreneur in his new business venture. It was a dream about the painful past. There was no real story line, but he knew how the tale ended. He saw images of Gwyn in bed and of IV drips and heart monitors flatlining. A hand gripped his, then let go. As he saw his face flooding with tears, the conductor's screechy intercom voice shook him out of his painful reverie. Next stop would be the last, he said, and the train would be going into the yard.

"All passengers must exit," the conductor warned as lights began to flash, signaling the closing of the car's doors.

Barnaby leapt from his seat and had to stop the doors from crushing him to make it out in time for his stop. He tripped on the gap that signs everywhere warned passengers to watch, but he righted himself without falling down or bumping into the train as it slowly pulled out. He walked dizzily along the stippled yellow rubber safety zone behind which passengers were supposed stand as trains approached or departed. The moving train was only about six inches from his right arm, but he didn't seem to notice.

He mounted the stairs. Before he made his way to the parking lot exit, he felt a tap on his shoulder. His shoulders fell in despair and he tensed, ready to be the target of more twitchy anger. But it wasn't Dora. For a minute, he thought he was still in his dream and it was Gwyn come to life, but it was a friendly, familiar face: Barbara Wade, a good friend of his wife who looked a lot like her and was even the same size.

Barbara did a lot of charitable work in the village even though she didn't have much money herself. A retired hospice nurse, she ran an informal caring committee for the local Methodist church. At Thanksgiving she called on people like Barnaby and Gwyn to provide turkey and other fixings for needy families in the village, many of whom were immigrants from Latin America. At Christmas, she asked people to donate presents, usually warm clothes.

Barnaby and Gwyn usually signed up for two families. Since her death, Barnaby had kept up the tradition, usually buying the designated items in the requested sizes and colors, shopping online. He dropped them off personally at Barbara's house, which was only a few blocks east from his.

Barbara started to say something but coughed instead, the product of a nasty lifetime habit of cigarette smoking. Newports were her preferred poison, and Barnaby thought he detected a whiff of smoke emanating from her clothes as her body spasmodically tried to get rid of unwanted substances in her lungs.

Barbara finally collected herself, apologized and made her pitch. She was behind in arranging the deliveries for Thanksgiving, just days away, and wondered if Barnaby might be free that Saturday to help her with her list and calls to families that needed food. It was a job Gwyn had volunteered for in the past. He found it hard to refuse Barbara and said yes. She gave him a hug that put the top of her head close to his face. The embrace startled Barnaby, partly because he detected a scent of Prell, the shampoo Gwyn had used.

When he got home, he went to the closet Gwyn had used. He took out a wool suit and ripped the plastic bag off it. He pressed the left shoulder to his nose. Surely dry cleaning fluid had erased any hint of Gwyn, but he nonetheless thought he detected something familiar. He hung the suit on the inside door handle of his bedroom and did the same with a dress and sweater from Gwyn's closet. A little something for Barbara on Saturday. He was pretty sure Gwyn would approve.

Chapter 14

On Saturday, Barnaby was up by seven. He showered and had his usual pancake breakfast by eight. That seemed too early to call on Barbara so he decided to head to the point for a nice walk and some birding. He'd hoped to spot bald eagles scanning the Hudson's waters for a meal. But they still weren't there. It hadn't gotten cold enough, Barnaby guessed.

The weather had sent the swans and Great Blue Herons south but not the annoying flocks of Canada geese. Like cockroaches, they were scouring the ground for grains and grubs, pooping everywhere as they did. Barnaby was fond of most birds, but he sometimes wished that a great plague would rid the region of the befouling pests. As he drove past them, he had a fantasy about using Victor's pistol some early morning. "Pow, Pow," he said to himself, using his right thumb and index finger as a fake gun pointed at the birds.

He drove to the upper lot and checked for nocturnal owls sleeping in the branches of nearby pine trees but found none. Word was that a Great Horned Owl that inhabited the park farther west had wiped out the gentler short-eared breed. Sometimes it was a cruel world, Barnaby thought, casting his assessment to things beyond the fate of birds.

He headed past the remnants of the RV crowd. Some campers stayed through December or even longer, perhaps to take advantage of the cheap rent. He walked past the flimsy wooden brown cabins that housed vacationers in the summer and sometimes families of the prison guards of Sing Sing in colder months.

He strolled toward the historic English Yews that had been planted in the 19th Century by a doctor who lived in a mansion on the point, once an Indian midden thanks to the abundance of shellfish in the shallows of the Hudson.

He didn't have much luck spotting wildlife, other than some frisky gray squirrels using the tree limbs of oaks and maples as highways to haul acorns to winter larders. In luckier visits, he'd seen American Pipits, Horned Larks, and even a Lapland Longspur. The area was birder heaven, which made it popular with the eagles and other raptors. They'd prey on their winged cousins when the fishing wasn't good. The only ones that gave the raptors a hard time were the feisty gulls, who voyaged up the so-called Atlantic Flyway to scavenge along the estuary as it ebbed and flowed from New York City to Albany.

Barnaby took a few pictures of the Tappan Zee Bridge in the distance when he got to land's end, then headed back home, using a lower dirt trail to get to the parking lot. Well along the path, with a dense stand of trees to his left, he stopped in his tracks. High on a limb about 40 feet above was an owl looking right at him with its unique yellow eyes. A daytime owl, hunting while its relatives slept. The owl was white and about two feet tall. Barnaby instantly realized what it was. He'd been reading birding blogs for weeks about how the strange arctic weather was pushing the rare Snowy Owl farther into the United States than usual.

The migration, perhaps triggered by a drop in the population of lemmings, the powerful hunters' preferred diet, was called an irruption, he'd read. One of the owls had been spotted in Boston the week before, and here was another, or perhaps the same one, perched before him.

Barnaby had only brought his point-and-shoot camera. It had a modest zoom lens and he snapped the bird as best he could. Maybe with some manipulation and a little help from Tesla he would have a nice shot for his collection. He took out his life-list book from his shoulder bag and recorded the time and place of his sighting, his first ever for the species.

In a month of surprises, some of them nasty, his old hobby had trumped his new one with this gift. Or was it a bad omen, he asked himself as he closed the book. White species of anything usually had weird tales associated with them. The mother of them all, of course, was Moby Dick. He hoped that wouldn't be the parallel.

Barnaby tried to take another good shot, but the owl took off north before he could. All he got was a close-up of the bird's tail as it disappeared behind the trees. Barnaby strolled back to his car, thinking fondly about his digitally-captured prize and was back home in a quarter of an hour. He downloaded the images from his morning session, blowing up the image of the owl to full size on his computer and made it his desktop wallpaper. He printed out a copy for Tesla, who was a fan of the Harry Potter books. Harry's faithful companion Hedwig was a Snowy Owl, and he was sure Tesla would treasure his image of the real-life thing.

Barnaby suddenly remembered he'd promised to help Barbara with the Thanksgiving meals for the less fortunate of his village. He closed down his computer and raced out of the house, after grabbing the collection of Gwyn's clothes he'd set aside the night before.

Barbara's house was a one-story structure made of wood, which she painted white except for the faux forest-green shutters. There was a garage to the right of the front entrance, but Barbara kept her decade-old Honda in the driveway on most days at the end of the year, using the garage space for food supplies for Thanksgiving and presents for Christmas. Poor families who celebrated other end-of-year holidays were eligible for help from the caring committee, but it was mostly a Christian affair, run by an ecumenical committee of believers in Christ and intended for those who had been baptized. Barbara made no such distinction.

Though she used the local Methodist church for her meals and presents drives, Barbara herself was an Episcopalian. She was a member of the choir and handed out readings of the day at the church door or helped collect donations from the dwindling flock. Shortly before Halloween each year, though, she dropped out of church work and barely made it to Sunday services as she threw herself into the gift-giving that consumed her life at the end of the year.

Barnaby brought along a frozen turkey that he'd gotten for free at the local supermarket. He'd stocked up on provisions the weekend before so his bill would qualify him for a free turkey in the store's annual promotion. It was the smart move. With the turkey costing nothing, he had more to spend on pumpkin pies, butternut squash, readymade bread stuffing and cranberries.

Barbara's house looked like an army field kitchen, with orders laid out on every available surface, including the dresser in her bedroom. Barnaby was joined by three other residents of his village whom he'd met before when he and Gwyn had come over on similar Saturdays before she died.

Looking at Barbara, Barnaby occasionally had flashbacks to his wife when she was alive. She and Barbara roughly looked alike if one didn't make too careful an examination. In demeanor and determination they could have been sisters, which might explain why they'd been good friends. The key distinguishing thing about Barbara that set her apart from Gwynn was that she smoked. A Newport dangled from her lips as she fielded telephone calls that Saturday and barked out orders to Barnaby and the others on what to take to which family. The only thing that slowed her pace was the frequent pause to cough, an exhalation that seemed to come from deep in her lungs, with hints of malignant wetness at its origins.

"Don't say it," she said to Barnaby at one point when she caught him watching her during one of her coughing fits. "I know I'm going to die if I don't stop it, but I just can't, so I'm going to live as much as I can till I can't."

Barnaby just nodded his head, offering no criticism or counterpoint. Her ill health once again brought back all the gut-wrenching tragedy of his wife's last days. Clothespins, then Barbara coughing. It was the unpredictable things that undid him. He again did what he always did when the suppressed memory screamed back into his thoughts. He willed his focus back to the task at hand. There was nothing he could do to change the past, he knew. He must look forward. That was not only the smart move. It was what Gwyn would have wanted.

By the end of the day, Barbara's volunteer crew had delivered all their parcels to their intended beneficiaries. Barnaby's goods were delivered by someone else, which was one of Barbara's rules: keep it professional; don't get too involved in talking to the families lest they get embarrassed.

As it turned out, Barnaby had the last run of the day because his family hadn't been home when he got there. He'd had to wait for them in their building's parking lot. That was another Barbara rule. Don't leave gifts on the porch or inside the storm door. They'll get stolen, as some had early on in the tradition. Needy didn't necessarily mean honest, she'd told him.

Barbara was sitting on a stool in her kitchen, having cleaned up the boxes and string and papers from the day's mission.

Dressed in a belted cardigan, she had what looked like a scotch in a short glass next to her and had another cigarette in her mouth. Despite the trail of smoke from the Newport, Barnaby smelled something aromatic in the air and saw that the oven was on.

"Meatloaf," Barbara said after she spotted him looking toward the stove. "Want some?"

Barnaby didn't answer at first.

"I could use the company," she said before he could respond.

Barnaby agreed to stay and share the meal, not exactly sure why since he had a perfectly acceptable casserole in a large Tupperware container in his fridge. He helped set the kitchen table with cutlery and paper napkins. Barbara got a bottle of wine from some other room and put it on the table with a thud.

"We earned it," she said.

A metal lid on a small pot began rattling as the steam escaped after the water inside came to a boil.

"Green beans," she said. "Nothing too fancy, but pretty tasty with a little butter and salt."

Barbara and Barnaby ate without a lot of conversation at first, but after each had had a glass of the wine, the topics turned to caring committee work that had to be done before Christmas.

"Could you do three families this year?" Barbara asked. "I'm running out of Good Samaritans."

Barnaby should have hesitated about taking on more financial responsibility after his layoff, but he said, "I guess."

"I wouldn't ask, but two of my best donors died over the summer, and I fear I'm not far behind."

"Let's hope not."

Barbara shooed away the sentiment with her left arm as she used her right to take another drink.

"Just being realistic. Next year I may be on the caring-committee list myself." She took another sip of wine. "If I'm lucky to live that long."

Before Barnaby could protest again, Barbara shot out of her chair and started clearing dishes and putting them in the dishwasher. Barnaby helped, as he used to do when Gwyn was alive. When they were done, they took what was left of the wine into her living room. Barbara had a small brick fireplace that was already stocked with wood and paper. She crouched down, took out a butane lighter from her sweater pocket and lit the starter paper. After the flame took hold, she sat in one of her arm chairs and watched the fire spread through the wood and became a nice blaze.

Barnaby had taken a seat on Barbara's couch. The TV remote was on the coffee table in front of him. Barbara asked him to see what was on TV. He flicked through the channels before finding the start of a Seinfeld episode.

"That's is a good one," Barbara said. "Stop there."

Barnaby had seen it too, a couple of times with Gwyn. Everything suddenly seemed to be a reminder of her, and being at Barbara's wasn't helping any. Five minutes into the episode, which was set mostly in a coffee shop, Barbara began coughing. The spasm was more violent that before. She took out a cloth handkerchief from her other sweater pocket. She tried to use it to suppress the coughing. After four more coughs, Barbara was able to catch her breath. She wiped her mouth with the handkerchief and put it back in her pocket but not before Barnaby noticed a small stain of black blood on it.

"You all right?" he asked.

"Yeah," she said without much emphasis.

She stood up creakily, using the stuffed chair's arms for leverage. After she was able to stand erect in front of it, she fainted.

Barnaby rushed over. He had his cell phone in his jacket and sprinted to get it, planning to dial 911. He punched in the numbers on his way back to Barbara, but before he hit the send button, she was conscious again and attempting to sit up.

"What happened?" she asked.

"You fainted. I was about to call an ambulance."

Barbara's eyes narrowed in pain.

"Don't do that. Just help me get into bed."

"You sure?"

"Yes. This has happened before. It passes."

Barnaby gave Barbara a supporting arm as she walked to her bedroom. She managed to get into the bathroom without help. He heard her brushing her teeth, and a toilet flushed. She came out wearing a nightgown under a thin robe. She went over to her bed and sat down. She was in her bare feet. Barnaby noticed her bunny slippers were neatly stored next to the side of the queen-size bed she was sitting on. She slipped her arms out of the robe and Barnaby took it from her and folded it.

"Just set it on the floor. I may need it tonight."

Barbara slipped under the covers, and Barnaby tucked her in as if she were a small child.

"What does your doctor say?"

Barbara managed a small smile.

"You don't want to know."

"You sure? Be happy to be a sounding board."

Barbara breathed in deeply and let the air out slowly before responding.

"I'm going to die."

"Oh, Barbara."

"But not for a while. In the meantime, it's going to be painful."

"Can't you get painkillers?"

"Had a bunch already. Enough for the whole village. But I'm just becoming a junkie, and pretty soon I'll be a zombie, so who wants that?"

"Can't you stop smoking?"

"I literally can't. Tried it many times. Even if I could, it's too late. I waited too long to see the doctor, so now my best-case scenario is that I last through Christmas so I can get all the committee presents delivered. Then it will be somebody else's problem. Maybe yours."

"No one could replace you, Barbara."

"Someone will have to."

Barbara starting coughing again, as violently as before. She reached out to a tissue box on her nightstand and pulled out a couple of Kleenex. As before, when she was done with the spasms, there was blood on the tissue after she had wiped her mouth.

"You sure you're OK?"

She shook her head.

"Getting worse every day."

"Anything I can do?"

Barbara hesitated then asked: "Would you stay with me the night? If I die, I don't want it to be alone."

"Don't be silly. You're not going to die tonight. You've got too much to do."

Barbara managed a thin smile.

"That's what Gwyn would have said. She was pretty brave at the end too, wasn't she?"

Barnaby didn't answer at first, then said, "Yes. Yes, she was."

"Just sit next to me till I fall asleep, would you?"

Barnaby slowly crawled into the bed, situating himself on top of the comforter on the left side of the bed, leaving his shoes on. He plumped the pillows behind him so he could sit up straight.

Barbara reached over and turned out her nightstand light and closed her eyes.

Barnaby tried not to close his eyes, planning to leave as soon as Barbara had fallen asleep. After ten minutes in the dark, he found himself getting drowsy and his lids began to flutter involuntarily. Suddenly he felt Barbara grasp his right hand with her left. His body stiffened not sure what she wanted. But in a minute or two he could hear a gentle snore. He knew he could slip out of the bed, but he didn't. He daydreamed about Gwyn for a while, remembering how they had slept in his own queen-size bed not so long before. The daydream turned into a real one and the next thing he knew he heard birdsong.

Barnaby made breakfast. Barbara dragged herself out of the bedroom and picked at his scrambled eggs.

"I should go," he said.

"Thanks for staying."

"Anyone would have."

"No, anyone would not have."

Barbara kissed Barnaby on the cheek.

He moved toward the door to leave.

"Hey, wait a minute," she said in a raspy voice.

She went into her dining room and came back with a slip of paper with names n it.

"Your Christmas families. Never too early to get started."

As Barnaby left, Mr. Bo hit a dozing Mr. Xi in the shoulder to alert him to start the engine of their surveillance car.

"He's coming out," Bo said.

"About time. I can't believe he stayed the night with that woman. Just the image of those two in bed."

"Forget that. John should have let us shoot him a week ago."

"He had to get clearance."

"That takes a week?"

"We had that meth job anyway. Guarding those shipments was more important than this clown."

"I'd still would have shot him last night. Then we wouldn't have had to spend the night in the van."

Chapter 15

Barnaby was home a few minutes later. He went to his kitchen to check his voice mail from the wall phone. Before he could, he spotted Tesla in his back yard, using the straw archery target he'd set up for her in the summer. He went outside and saw she'd put four arrows in the bull's eye at the far end of the grass.

"Hey, Mr. G. Hope you don't mind my practicing."

"No, no. Anytime. That's why we set it up."

"I'm getting pretty good. I was thinking maybe I could train for the Olympics. But their target is about twice as far away as that one. Bull's eye looks like a thumb tack."

"Why not?? Barnaby said, glad to have a happier topic to discuss than the one he'd just left at Barbara's house. "I think you could do it."

"Geena Davis, the actress. She picked it up pretty fast and made the team a while back. You know, the Thelma and Louise one."

"Oh, yeah. And don't forget the Amazons. They were great at it."

"Yeah, but they cut off one boob so it wouldn't get in the way of the bowstring...No way I'm doing that."

Barnaby cleared his throat.

"I don't think that's an Olympic requirement."

Tesla laughed.

"Probably not. But this bow isn't Olympic-issue either. I need something better. Got this one on EBay. Owner broke his arm."

"It's pretty with those curves at the end. Reminds me of the ones on Greek vases."

"Yeah, the Greeks used them. They're called recurved bows. Give you a lot of extra distance compared with straight ones."

"Well, if you need some help buying the right bow, let me know."

"Nah. You've done enough. You and Mrs. G. She got me my first bow back when I was in Scouts. Remember?"

"I remember. A little red wooden thing, wasn't it?"

"Yeah. I'd probably break it if I pulled back on it now, but if I get into a good college and make the archery team, they should supply the real deal. But for now, it'll just be a hobby."

A safer one than I've chosen, Barnaby thought, as Tesla pulled the bow's string back to her right eye with about 40 pounds of draw weight and put another steel-tipped arrow into the target, dead-center.

*　*　*

On Monday, Barnaby went into the city. It was a teacher's holiday at the high school, and he asked Tesla to come along as his assistant, promising $10 an hour, including travel time. It was raining, so he drove to the station, figuring the cost of parking, discounted for village residents, would be less than sending his soaked, wrinkled clothes to the cleaners at the end of the day. He took the 9:45 a.m. semi-express so he didn't see any of his regulars. He had an appointment with Victor at the garment factory at eleven. He calculated he could make it on time by taxi or even with a brisk, no-cost walk from Grand Central if the rain stopped. The sun had poked through scattered rain clouds by the time he and Tesla got to Grand Central, and they made it on foot to the factory with about a minute to spare. Barnaby introduced Tesla.

"Who's she? Your date?" Jerzy asked.

"She's my assistant," Barnaby said.

"They got laws against that kind of thing," said Jerzy's co-worker, whose uniform shirt said his name was "Duke." "Don't go crossing any state lines."

Jerzy laughed as Victor watched in silent amusement. Tesla didn't say anything.

"She's an expert on computers," Barnaby said, sounding irritated. "And she's on the payroll. Strictly professional."

"What kind of profession we talking about?' Jerzy said.

"All right, boys," Victor interrupted. "Knock it off. She's Mr. Gilbert's guest, so zip it."

Victor waited a moment as he stared at Tesla.

"So what kind of name is Tesla?"

"Serbian."

"You Serbian?"

"No. Just named after one."

"Who's that?"

"Nikola Tesla. He was a famous inventor."

"Never heard of him."

"He's responsible for AC electricity. And radio."

"Radio? Thought that was Marconi. At least that's what my Italian grandmother told me."

"Lot of people think that because Marconi won the Nobel for radio. But later, it was proven Tesla invented it first."

"And so your parents named you after this guy?"

"No. I did that. When I was about seven."

"You named yourself?"

"My real name is Hortense. After my grandmother. I loved her, but, well, you know."

Victor nodded and said: "Nuff said. Hor's not much of a nickname."

As the conversation petered out, Barnaby took the opportunity to present his plans to streamline Victor's manufacturing operations. When it got to be noontime, Victor told Duke to get some sandwiches. He came back with Italian combos from a local deli. Jerzy got some bottles of wine from the office. Victor poured a Puglia red into various, unmatched short glasses. He hesitated before doing one for Tesla but gave her a half measure. She took a sip without any hesitation.

By one o'clock, they were done eating, having discussed some offseason baseball trades and the Giants and Jets chances to make the Super Bowl. As Duke came around with a plastic garbage bag to collect everyone's lunch trash, Barnaby brought out another folder from his brief case and directed his attention to Victor.

"I know it's not part of my assignment, but I had a couple of thoughts about your computer business upstairs. Actually Tesla did."

Victor's looked irked.

"I know I don't know much about it," Barnaby said, noticing Victor's reaction. "But any business that uses computers, no matter what it is, has some inherent inefficiencies, and I've gone over the matter with my, uh, assistant."

"Ass-istant," Jerzy said.

"Jerzy!" Victor said.

Tesla kept a poker face and said nothing.

"Go on," Victor said.

"Thanks," Barnaby said. "I think you'll find this interesting. Tesla is a real genius when it comes to computers. If she weren't so honest, she could be quite the hacker."

"Wouldn't let her to do that," Victor said. 'That's criminal, you know."

"I'm well aware of that, and the good news is that she knows a lot about how to stop the crooks — and who they are."

"Hmm," Victor said. "Tell me more."

"Well, the pure crooks are mostly Eastern European, though the Chinese are very busy trying to steal patents and merger data and that kind of thing. But it's more of an industrial or economic policy for them — to give them an edge over us."

"Eastern European, huh? Do you know precisely who, Tesla?"

"They're pretty hard to trace," Tesla said. "Even if you do, the authorities in Ukraine or wherever aren't too helpful."

"Yeah, it's terrible what goes on over there. In the Ukraine, I mean. My poor father must be rolling over in his grave."

"You can at least stop them," Tesla said.

"Un huh."

"That's why we worked up a number of things you might want to consider to improve security and streamline your network. A better firewall, more complex passwords – numbers and letters and some symbols, like a dollar sign — fingerprint IDs, and a backup randomly selected number code you have to type in. But you'd need a little device for that."

"And what have you figured out about my business, Barnaby?"

"Nothing much. Except that you use computers a lot. What is it you do?"

A smile.

"I guess you could say sales. We try to get people to go to Web sites, and we collect money for each time they visit."

For Tesla, the explanation triggered a memory of what her cyber-security friend Veronica had told her about botnets and Eastern European hackers.

"How do you get them to visit?" Barnaby asked.

"That's sort of a trade secret."

Victor changed the subject before Barnaby got too interested in what the computer operation did. He asked Barnaby if he would do a favor for him.

"Sure. Anything"

"Anything?"

"Well, I guess I didn't mean anything literally. You're my first client. So I meant 'anything' if it's not too dangerous – and not illegal, of course."

"Of course. This would be just business. In this case, Jerzy's business."

Jerzy got a surprised look on his face.

"I'm just asking because he's in a bind," Victor said, cocking his head toward Jerzy. "And he's a bit shy."

Jerzy nodded but said nothing.

Victor handed over a small zipped tote bag and a thick Manila envelope. He handed Barnaby a business card with Chinese ideographs and an address in English that Barnaby calculated was in Chinatown.

"You take this stuff to that address and hand over that card, and a man named Mr. Deng will take this stuff and give you a different envelope."

Barnaby nodded and said: "OK."

Victor handed over another business card with an address in Elizabeth, New Jersey.

"Then take a cab. Jerzy will reimburse you. And give the new envelope to another Chinese gentleman. He's called Patrick. I don't get it, but that's what he's called."

"That's it?"

"Yep. He'd have his own guys do it, but they're really busy. Right, Jerzy?"

"Right, boss."

"Jerzy's got a little business on the side. I don't know a lot about it, but if this works out, maybe he'll want you to give him some advice too. Maybe even set up a delivery service for runs like this."

"Or outsource it," Barnaby said. "That might be cheaper."

Victor shook his head a bit.

"Not so sure about outsiders. He needs someone trustworthy. Like you. Right, Jerzy?"

Jerzy had been reading the New York Post and looked up suddenly.

"Yeah, sure."

After Barnaby and Tesla left, Jerzy asked if it was a good idea to give Barnaby the package of cash and phony customs documents.

"If that shipment of Nikes, Coach and Juicy goods comes through with no trouble, then we'll know we can trust him. And he's made himself an official co-conspirator for smuggling counterfeit goods and money laundering."

"And if not?"

"It's not a big shipment. No cigarettes, no meth. But if the cops show up, then Mr. Gilbert is dead meat."

*　*　*

The exchange of envelopes in Chinatown didn't take long. Mr. Deng, a man in his 50s who dressed in an old-fashioned Chinese suit, came out quickly from the back office of a grocery store after Barnaby handed over the business card to the cashier.

"New man?" Deng asked.

"Beg your pardon?"

"I haven't seen you before on this run."

"Ah, yes. New man. Just doing a colleague a favor."

Deng opened the packet at one end, showing what looked like bound stacks of cash.

"Must be a trusting colleague," Deng said.

Barnaby and Tesla hailed a cab after the envelope switch and headed toward the address Victor had given Barnaby for a site at the Port Newark-Elizabeth Marine Terminal. On the way, Tesla opened the envelope and pulled out a packet of filled-in customs forms describing goods delivered by container ship.

"Looks like a lot of designer stuff," she said, snapping Barnaby out of a daydream that had the Manhattan skyline as a backdrop.

"I don't think you should have looked in there, Tesla. We're just messengers. It's none of our business."

"Maybe. But a lot of times it's the messenger who gets killed."

Chapter 16

The address number was crudely painted on a small wooden board bolted to a chain-link fence gate. Barnaby told a guard on the other side that he had an appointment with Patrick. He was let through to a zone of warehouses and whizzing forklifts. The guard told him to wait for an escort. As Barnaby did, he tried to place the stink in the air. Some sort of chemical, he guessed, trying not to inhale too much.

The escort, a white man in a denim shirt and jeans, led Barnaby and Tesla to a warehouse office about a quarter of a mile from the gate. The man called Patrick, who had a thin mustache and wore Ray-Ban sunglasses, was seated at a metal desk and remained in his chair as he signaled with impatient fingers for Barnaby to give him the envelope. He examined the contents, and, after a moment looked up. As if suddenly noticing Tesla, he asked: "Who's the chick?"

"Ah, she's my niece. Just along for the ride."

Patrick, who wore a red flannel shirt under denim overalls, smiled and said: "Niece? That's good. Nice cover."

* * *

During the cab ride back to Manhattan, Barnaby apologized to Tesla for all the wisecracks about her being his girlfriend.

"No big deal, Mr. G. Lot of jerks in the world."

"Well, I'm glad you're taking it so calmly. I mean, it's just such a ridiculous concept. A girl of your age."

"You'd be surprised what girls of my age get up to these days, Mr. G."

Barnaby nodded, thinking of Dora.

By the time the cab made it through the Holland Tunnel, Barnaby saw they could make it to Grand Central in time for an early rush hour train back home. Barnaby and Tesla got facing seats in one of the newer cars so they both had a view of the river. Barnaby looked around and didn't see any of his regulars. But at 125th Street, a familiar woman in her forties entered the car. It was the hennaed-haired women he called Helga. She took a window seat just a few rows back from where Barnaby was sitting. He was facing backwards, so he had a full view of her without having to turn around. She wore her hair in a mannish cut, chopped just below her ear lobes, like Greta Garbo in Ninotchka. She was dressed in a gray pinstriped suit and had a dark khaki trench coat that was unbuttoned to show a medium blue blouse with a loosely knotted maroon tie — a sort of power suit ensemble. She sported fitted kid leather gloves that matched her shoes and had a shoulder bag with a Gucci logo. Barnaby wondered if it was the real thing or if she had made a trip to Canal Street and met Jasmine Leung.

He chatted with Tesla for a while about getting a new computer, though he was listening more than contributing to the conversation. Barnaby found himself glancing at the woman a number of times. On a couple of those occasions, he saw her look up from her leather-bound book and stare at him. He'd never talked to the woman, but he'd always been curious about her. Maybe even slightly attracted. He wasn't sure why.

Except in the worst of weather, the woman had the habit of commuting to the station by bicycle, a vintage three-speed model. Before riding home, she would change out of her pumps, which usually had spiked heels. She'd put on flat black trainers that had three stripes on each side. She had a basket on the front of the bicycle where she placed her purse for the ride home. He wondered if she'd ridden to the station in the morning, when it was raining. As it turned out, she had.

When the train pulled into Barnaby's stop, the woman got up first and was at the exit door before Barnaby and Tesla lined up. She didn't turn around, but Barnaby saw her reflection in the door glass and sensed she was using that ersatz mirror to look back at him. His inclination was to go home, but he found he had an urge to follow the woman. It wasn't the logical thing to do, but he found the temptation irresistible. He told Tesla he'd be home shortly.

He'd discussed his new hobby with Tesla. It was hardly a secret given the files he'd been keeping on his hacked and borrowed computers. Tesla hadn't judged him on his whimsy, despite the bizarre adventures he'd had up to then.

"Maybe this one will be a little more normal," Tesla said, looking at the woman as she cycled away. "There have to be some normal people in the New York area."

"Exactly. I'm going to have a positive mental attitude about it. The old PMA."

The woman was easy to follow. The route she took was uphill most of the way, so he'd caught up with her not long after he got into his car and took off in pursuit. She didn't live far from the station. A bit long for a walk, but just about right for a bike ride. A smart move in time and money, Barnaby thought. A kindred spirit?

Her house had a peaked roof with a short side on the left as you faced it and a sloping long one on the right that finished off with a small tail that created an eave. The windows were of a casement variety with small panes. The frames were black and stood out tastefully against the gray stucco façade. There was no garage and no car in the driveway, though there was a late model charcoal Infiniti convertible with black leather seats parked in front.

The woman was in the process of bringing her bicycle into a side door at the end of the house's macadam driveway when she spotted Barnaby's car, which he'd stopped in front to observe his subject. It's what he would have done if he'd been tracking some bird, but as he'd found out the hard way in his new pursuit, people were different from birds. Barnaby had taken out his point-and-shoot camera in case he wanted to snap some shots of the woman. It was lying on the passenger seat when the woman dropped her bike on the ground and strode toward him. When she got to his car, she made a circular motion with her hand as if ordering him to roll down the window. Barnaby hit the right power-window button and the glass on the passenger side disappeared into the door.

"Get out," the woman said. Spotting the camera, she added: "Bring your camera. It might come in handy."

Barnaby was so flummoxed by the woman's reaction that he parked his car in front of the convertible, closed the window, grabbed his camera and got out of his car.

"I had a feeling about you on the train," she said, after he got out and walked up to her.

She led him to her side door. Inside, she parked her bicycle in a mudroom to the right of the entrance and walked into the kitchen. Barnaby was right behind. The woman opened the refrigerator door and took out a bottle of white wine. It had a rubber cork in it. Air whooshed out of the neck when the woman uncorked it. It was the same wine-saving device Barnaby used, he noticed. She poured herself a glass but didn't offer Barnaby any.

"I charge $200 for the first visit," she said. "It may go up af-ter I find out what you like."

"I'm not following you."

"Oh, you will. Believe me, you will."

The woman took a sip from her wine glass and put it on the marble countertop near her gas-stove top.

"Take off your coat. Let's see what we have."

Barnaby, wanting to be polite, did as he was told, putting his trench coat over the back of a tall counter chair. He was wear-ing a camel-colored sports coat over a light blue shirt and black gabardine slacks. His tie shoes were of the comfortable dress ca-sual variety that looked good enough for business meetings but were just the thing for any long walks that became necessary.

"Aren't you a vision," the woman said after inspecting Barn-aby's wardrobe. "Very buttoned up. Land's End or Joseph A. Bank?"

"A little of both," Barnaby said, sounding a bit defensive as predator and prey roles seemed to be getting reversed. "They're good for business casual,"

"Casual isn't my preference. I'm a little stricter than that."

"Your suit is very professional. Are you a professional?"

"Very."

"I'm sure I missed something, but what is it you do for the $200? I'm not really in the market for anything at the moment, but I am curious what you do. You see that's why I followed you."

The woman's forehead crinkled at the remark.

"It's sort of a hobby," Barnaby said. "I follow people who ride my train to see where they go."

The woman stared but continued to say nothing.

"It's sort of like bird watching – but with people."

The woman, who was circling Barnaby, nodded her head as she took that in.

"Innocence. That's good. We can work with that."

"I'm not sure what you mean."

"Did someone refer you to me or did we just connect?"

"Ah, I guess we connected. I'd seen you riding your bike. It just made me curious."

"Uh huh."

"You're not the first."

"I'll bet. But I think you'll find I'll be the best."

Barnaby swallowed so that it could be heard.

"Well, I love a good story, and I've heard some corkers recently. You have no idea what some of the people on the train do. I bet you'd be surprised."

"Usually my clients are the ones who are surprised."

"About what?"

"Their limits."

Barnaby nodded his head as he computed that.

"So you're a consultant?" he asked.

The woman laughed as she threw her head back.

"More like a boss. People come to me because they want to be told what to do."

"You must be very good then if they just do it blindly."

"Sometimes they literally do it blindly. Does that interest you?"

"Well, I'm not really in the market for a consultant. In fact I'm sort of a consultant myself."

The woman grimaced.

"I find that hard to believe."

She took another sip of wine and moved toward Barnaby. She moved her hands to his jacket lapels and stripped it off him in one deft move, letting it fall to the floor.

"Before we start," she said, "I like to establish a 'safe word.' I take you have one."

"Not that I know of."

"We could just use 'Uncle!' People seem to remember that one from childhood and shout it out if things get a little too intense."

Barnaby blinked his eyes in befuddlement.

"Now I'm really not following you. What kind of consulting could get that intense? Are you like a therapist or something?"

The woman smiled.

"People do find what I do very therapeutic. Why don't you sit down on that hard chair over there? I'll be right back. I need to get some equipment. Mostly I do this at my studio in the city, but I have some backup things here."

The woman took a while before she came back with a plastic box full of ropes, dog collars and some other devices that confused Barnaby further. She had changed out of her business suit into leather pants and a black silk blouse that was buttoned all the way to the top.

"Sometimes people like a little something to calm them down a bit, to break the ice so to speak, but if you've done this before, perhaps you want to be fully conscious to enjoy the session.

"I'm not really ready for any session, whatever it is you do."

Barnaby looked at the box of gear the woman had brought out. He noticed it included a coiled whip.

"Are you like an animal trainer or something."

The woman took out the whip and cracked it, making Barnaby wince.

"That's good. I like the persona you're using."

The woman tossed the whip aside, came up to Barnaby and grabbed his shirt with her right hand just under his neck, making him rise a bit in the chair.

"Stay still. Don't move unless I tell you."

Barnaby's eyes widened.

"I think there has been some terrible misunderstanding, and besides I don't have $200 with me. Maybe I could come back."

The woman let go of Barnaby's neck and stepped back.

"Don't break the mood. This was so promising."

"Well maybe you could send me an e-mail with the details of your services so I could have a better idea of what it is you do. I wouldn't want to waste your time."

Barnaby mustered his courage and got up from his chair. He grabbed his coats and his camera and headed for the side door in his shirtsleeves. The woman seemed stunned that Barnaby had shown such independence. He sprinted to his car. As he looked at the house from the driver's seat, he noticed the woman was at a front room window taking a picture of his car with a camera with a telephoto lens.

"Maybe she's a birder," he said to himself.

The woman put her camera on the kitchen counter after getting off a few more shots as Barnaby took off. She went to a closet off the bedroom and pushed the rewind button on a DVD machine installed there and watched a recording of her encounter with Barnaby. Not sure what to make of it, she checked the digital image on her camera and saw she'd captured Barnaby's tag number. She made a call to a town house in Harlem and asked for Selma.

After a brief explanation she asked her colleague to have the tag number checked.

"What do you think he was up to?"

"Either he's a cop or a complete idiot."

*   *   *

Later that afternoon, arriving on her usual train, Dora Pivo took the same route from the station as Barnaby had in following the henna-haired woman on the bicycle. The exact same route. She walked up the macadam driveway of a stucco house and entered the kitchen door without knocking.

"Hey, Aunty Kristal."

"Hey yourself, Dora," Kristal Power said as she was mixing herself a very dry martini.

She held up the stemmed glass and asked: "Want one?"

Dora crinkled her nose.

"A little early for me."

"Good day?" Kristal asked.

"Not bad. Learning the business."

Kristal raised her glass in a toast.

"Well when your dad makes you Selma's boss, and you're deciding your cut of my business down there, remember that this humble working girl was the one who gave you a place to stay so you could be close to your daddy."

"Not forgotten. Nice cover."

Kristal looked out the window as if thinking about something.

"I do miss those PTA meetings." Kristal smiled. "I got to be so bossy."

* * *

Barnaby found he had a voice mail from Barbara when he got back from his unnerving encounter with Kristal Power. Barbara sounded in pain and asked if he could stop by. He told Tesla he'd be back shortly. But he didn't come back that night.

Barbara's door was cracked open half an inch, and he went in after she didn't answer her bell, a series knocks or a loud "Hello." He didn't find her until he'd made his way back to her bedroom. She was sitting up in her bed with two pillows behind her back. Her eyes were closed when he first spotted her, but they opened slowly after he called her name. She said nothing, and he went over to the side of her bed.

"Can I get you something?" he asked.

After a pause, she said weakly, "Just a glass of water."

He got one from the kitchen and had to help her drink it.

"Can you stay the night again?" she asked after she'd finished. "Just in case I might need to go to the hospital in a hurry?"

Barnaby nodded and said he had to make a call. He telephoned Tesla and said they'd have to put off the model-train session he'd promised her till another time. Barnaby went back to the bedroom and asked Barbara: "You need anything else?"

She waited a minute, then said, "You know, I could use some help getting to the bathroom."

Barnaby eased Barbara out of bed. She was in a cotton nightgown, and he could feel her ribs as he guided her to the toilet. He put the lid up and helped her sit down on the seat, getting the bottom of the nightgown out of the way as he did. He'd had to do the same with Gwyn many times, and he found himself again trying to blot out the memory of that long nightmare. He was not ready to be a caregiver again, however temporary, but he saw no way around it at that moment.

"Let me know when you're finished," he said. He closed the door behind him to give Barbara some privacy.

A moment later, he heard the toilet flush and Barbara said, "All clear."

He came back in. Barbara was still sitting on the toilet. He put his hands under her armpits and helped her stand up.

"Now what?"

Barbara sighed and said, "You think you could manage a shower. Or at least run a bath?"

Barnaby looked at the shower stall and the standalone tub. A shower would mean getting into the stall without or with his clothes on, so he walked over to the tub and started running the water. It was the smart move, he decided.

When the water was about two-thirds up the side of the tub, Barnaby turned the faucets off. Looking to the left, he saw Barbara standing next to the sink, leaning on one arm to steady herself. She inched over to the tub. She bent over and dipped a hand into the water.

"Just right," she said softly.

"So what now?" Barnaby asked, pretty sure what the answer was.

"Full Monty time, I guess," she said. "I'm so sorry to put you through this."

Barnaby helped Barbara out of her nightgown and put his hands under her armpits again to help her step into the bath. She sank down into the tub with her toes closest to the taps, which had a hand shower attachment that was cradled on a hook above the faucets. Barbara, whose wrinkled, white body was visible below the soapless water, asked Barnaby to switch the shower attachment on.

"Not too hot," she said. "I want to do my hair."

With the water running, Barbara doused her head. She reached to her right and grabbed a plastic bottle of shampoo and worked a handful of the amber liquid into her matted hair. After it was sudsy, she groped for the showerhead. Seeing her difficulty, Barnaby grabbed it, getting his right shirt sleeve soaked in the process. He rinsed the soap from her head as if she were a child having a bubble bath. He'd done the kind thing instinctively, but the flash of a similar scene with Gwyn hit him hard.

He blinked his eyes and made an effort to blot the image out. In another setting, there might have been a sexual, even kinky undercurrent to the scene. But Barnaby found it all too clinical.

Her hair rinsed, Barbara said she wanted to get out. Barnaby got a large bath sheet from a rack near the sink and helped her step onto a terrycloth bath rug next to the tub. As water from Barbara's body dripped onto the mat, he got another towel from the rack and helped her dry her hair.

Barbara moved to a stool near her sink and asked Barnaby to get her hairdryer and a wide-tooth comb out of the top drawer of a cabinet next to the sink. He plugged it in and flicked on the medium speed. Barbara took the comb and asked him to hold the dryer above her head as she ran the comb and her fingers through her hair. When it was dry, she turned to check out her handiwork in the mirror.

"Beyond the call of duty, my dear. Way beyond."

Barnaby helped Barbara into her robe and then to bed. She said she was too tired to put on a nightgown and just wanted to get under the covers. She closed her eyes. Barnaby turned out the lights and hoped he wouldn't be asked to lie down next to Barbara again. She was silent as if the warm bath had already put her into an early slumber. Barnaby went out to the living room and flicked on the TV, putting the volume down low. He climbed into a recliner chair. Somewhere in the middle of the local cable news, he nodded off, too.

Again the pre-dawn birds awoke him gently. He usually could tell a finch from a grackle on any given day but the cacophony that morning — and maybe the situation —stumped him. He went to the kitchen and made some coffee.

Barbara had a coffee maker just like the one Gwyn had bought for their house. More painful thoughts of his wife's final months. Back, like a slide show, came the beeping hospital monitors and other mind-searing props of her demise. Barnaby gathered himself, as he usually was able to do, and brought a coffee into Barbara's bedroom. Her eyes opened as the aroma reached her. Again Barnaby had to help her drink. She pushed the coffee away before she was half finished and closed her eyes. After a few moments, Barnaby heard her gentle breaths that signaled her return to sleep.

With two coffees under his belt by seven-thirty, he peeked into her bedroom and saw she was still sleeping on her back, just as he had left her. He wrote her a note and left it on her nightstand, saying there was more coffee in the machine.

"Call if you need anything," he'd written, but he hoped she wouldn't.

Chapter 17

W hen Barnaby had called Tesla from Barbara's that night, Zoot Ames and Agent Urbanski were listening in thanks to the tap placed on Barnaby's phone.

"When the kid leaves, we can have a little look-see," Urbanski said.

Tesla came out of Barnaby's house about half an hour later, having done some work on his computer. After she'd passed them, Urbanski slipped out of the bureau surveillance van, which had the name of a tire-repair shop on the doors.

"Give me a holler if our boy scout shows up, and I'll high-tail it out the back."

"If I thought he was a boy scout, you wouldn't be going in there."

Urbanski, dressed in black windbreaker and blue jeans, made his way through Barnaby's side yard and found the storm door leading to the kitchen unlocked. He pulled out his leather case of picks and had the deadbolt lock on the kitchen door open in under a minute notwithstanding the hindrance of surgical gloves.

He pulled his mini-mag light from his right windbreaker pocket and made his way quickly to Barnaby's den. Urbanski inserted a thumb drive in the USB port of Barnaby's new computer and activated a download program to copy all files on the hard drive. He saw from the names that there were folders labeled Victor and Dora and John. The Victor folder seemed to be filled with documents about his businesses. There were other folders on birds, one of which was labeled Life List. There was an older one that read "Gwyn's Recipes" and a ton of photos that took a backup thumb drive to download.

As Victor's burglars had found, some files in unlabeled folders were encrypted. Urbanski installed an electronic listening device in the den and another in the kitchen in hopes of catching any conversations of interest that occurred without the use of a tapped phone. Getting no warning from Zoot at that point, he took a look around the house, finding it tidy with nothing untoward like a passport with foreign stamps or a weapon of some kind. Most of the floors were carpeted, and the kitchen was tiled, so there weren't any floorboards to pull up. No attic either. Just a crawl space. Not finding a handy ladder, Urbanski didn't go poking around up there. He made a quick trip to the basement and examined some of the train storage boxes from Barnaby's collection but didn't find anything incriminating there or in various boxes in the laundry room. He spotted the glass containers with Tesla's snakes and other pets, all of whom seemed to be dozing in the darkness, and just shook his head.

In less than half an hour he was back out the kitchen door, thankful for a dark back yard. Urbanski briefed Zoot on what he'd found — and hadn't. They decided to wait till Barnaby came home and turned to the unencrypted files while they waited.

"Wonder what's in those files?' Zoot asked.

"I know a couple of tricks a pal in the cyber-squad showed me. I'll give it a whirl. But otherwise I'll get him to open them in the morning."

Urbanski made half a dozen attempts to unlock the folders that were labeled only with numbers and letters. Frustrated, he used the folder numbers themselves as the passwords, but all that did was make the first file disappear.

"Whoa!" Urbanski said as it did. "What the hell happened?"

"Looks like Mr. Gilbert is unusually good with computers. Wonder who trained him."

"Somebody really good from the looks of this. Maybe he is working for the NSA."

"I still find that hard to believe."

"Whatever the deal, I'm going to have to scrub this whole unit down. I'm betting I just downloaded some virus."

*   *   *

When the sun came up, Urbanski drove the van to a Dunkin Donuts and got some coffee and a quick breakfast for the two of them. After a pit stop at the rest room, he and Zoot were back at Barnaby's house. A little after eight, Zoot rang the doorbell in case Barnaby had come home while they were away. Barnaby, just back from Barbara's, answered the door looking as disheveled as Zoot and Urbanski, all three having spent the night in their clothes. Zoot said it was nice to see Barnaby again and that he needed him to answer some questions.

"Now?" Barnaby said.

"Yeah, now," Urbanski said. "We didn't come to make an appointment."

Barnaby showed them into his living room, taking the main arm chair and gestured for the agents to use the sofa. Zoot noticed a large snake was sunning itself under a lamp on the far side of the couch but said nothing as he sat down on the side closest to Barnaby. Urbanski remained standing, his arms crossed, shooting looks at Herpie every once in a while.

"What do you know about this Vittorio Dragon guy you've been hanging around with lately?" Zoot asked.

Barnaby blinked at the question and after a moment said his relationship with Victor was confidential and that he was reluctant to share that kind of data.

"You may be sharing a cell with him if you're not more cooperative," Urbanski said. "Your pal Victor is a crook. Big time."

"I find that hard to believe. He's never given me any cause to suspect anything. And in his one payment for services so far, he paid in cash."

"I'll bet he did," Zoot said. "Victor's a cash kind of guy."

Barnaby remembered the cash he'd taken to Chinatown but decided to keep that detail to himself.

"Look, numbnuts, just answer our questions 'cause you're not his lawyer or priest, and last time I checked there was no legal privilege for conversations with a time expert or whatever it is you are."

"Time and motion. It's a recognized profession."

"Not by us."

Zoot turned to look at Urbanski, who stopped his taunts.

"Just tell us how you met Victor and what's happened since you did. And be completely truthful because if you lie, you'll find there are consequences. Criminal consequences."

"Well, if it's helping in an official investigation, I guess it wouldn't hurt. It's like being subpoenaed."

"Almost exactly," Urbanski said. "Next stop, grand jury."

Barnaby repeated his story about meeting Victor at his fish operation thanks to their using the same accountant. Barnaby told the agents of his advice to Victor about his fish business, including the suggestions about using frozen fish instead of tossing the live product out. He detailed the assistance he'd given him about rearranging the garment factory lines and what little he knew about the computers on the 8th floor.

"Computers?" Urbanski said.

"That would be new," Zoot added.

Zoot took notes during the interview, which he would type up into official bureau reports back at the office. Done with his questions for the moment, he clicked his pen closed and put it away in his inside jacket pocket. He stared at Barnaby a moment.

"It's an interesting story, but I'm still not sure whether to believe it."

"Why not?"

"As you yourself said, everyone you run into seems pretty weird or related or both. It just seems a bit too convenient, doesn't it?"

"As I explained, I followed the first one, and one thing led to another. A bit like hitting pool balls on the break. You never really know where they'll go."

"Somebody is going to be hitting your balls if you're holding back on us," Urbanski said.

Zoot's response wasn't as angry.

"There might be a way to prove your telling the truth."

"OK. As long as it's nothing illegal."

"We're the Federal Bureau of Investigation," Urbanski said. "If we're doing it, it's legal."

Barnaby nodded, remembering several news stories about agents who'd been arrested for acting illegally, but he kept that to himself. Zoot pulled out a small plastic box with another electronic component cradled inside on a foam rubber bed.

"Another bug?" Barnaby asked.

Zoot smiled and nodded.

"Yeah. Last ones you planted are working pretty well."

"Are you hearing what you expected?"

"Never mind what we're hearing," Urbanski said. "What we want you to do now is plant that little sucker in the office of the garment factory. From what you said, that seems the place private conversations might take place. Conversations not made on the phone."

"Like when Victor comes to visit the manager."

"Uh, huh," Barnaby said, thinking of the conversation he and Victor and Jerzy had had on the shop floor about Chinatown and the port and a shipment of imported goods — all discussed yards from the office. But he kept that too to himself, too.

"You just pull that piece of paper off the bottom and stick it on anything," Zoot said. "Underside of the desk. Behind some books in a bookcase. Somewhere where it won't be seen. It'll stay stuck like forever."

"Or till found."

Zoot shot Urbanski an angry look.

Barnaby swallowed hard and asked, "What if they do find it?"

Back and forth Zoot and Urbanski went like a tag team to persuade Barnaby to do their dirty work.

"Nothing to do with you," Zoot said. "They'll figure we got in there somehow or some law enforcement group. Or the Chinese."

"Right. Or the Chinese. We know they talk from what you said."

"Besides, you don't look like a cop, so they're not going to suspect you."

"But you can't let them see you plant it," Urbanski added.

"Yeah that would be bad, but you'll think of something. Ask to use the phone for a private call. Something like that."

Barnaby nodded as he heard the argument, then finally said: "OK. I can go down there tomorrow. I'll tell them I have to make a few more measurements or something."

"Yeah. Great. Lie."

"Just don't lie to us."

"How about the phone? Do I need to bug that?"

"That's covered," Urbanski said, glancing at Barnaby's living room phone.

Zoot shook Barnaby's hand on the way out.

"This'll be good."

"Yeah, it'll be exciting," Urbanski said. "Just like in the movies."

Barnaby nodded his head and looked again at the bug in the box. By the time he brought his head up, the agents were at the end of his sidewalk heading for their van.

"You ever get a warrant for the phone or that bug?" Urbanski asked.

Zoot grimaced.

"I want this to be our investigation. If I did all the paperwork, some other unit would bigfoot us and take it over. We're going to crack this one ourselves."

Urbanski thought about that.

"So if you get yourself back to organized crime, do I get to come along?"

Zoot smiled.

"I'll say I couldn't have done it without you."

"And what if our boy scout back there gets caught – or worse?"

"If it's worse, there's nothing to explain. He's dead. If it's something in between, he's just a lying co-conspirator trying to spin us. And this meeting we just had never actually happened. In the meantime, we got ourselves a confidential informant inside Victor's gang. We can write that up. No names. And take credit for whatever he gets."

"It's evil, but I like it."

Two other forces of evil had had to watch Barnaby's house from afar because Zoot and Urbanski had gotten the best spot first. Mr. Bo and Mr. Xi parked two blocks away and around the corner. Xi walked past the entrance to Barnaby's dead-end street periodically to monitor his activities. On one of the passes, he spotted the two agents coming out of the house.

"I think he's working for the bureau," Xi said when he returned to his surveillance car. "I saw that guy from the street again."

"That's up to John to decide."

"I'm tired of waiting! Let's call him now while Gilbert's alone."

"That is not a conversation we want to make on a cell phone."

Chapter 18

Zoot had Urbanski drop him off at home so he could shower and change clothes. His wife had already gone to work. The night before, he'd called her to say he'd be late, maybe really late, and not to wait up. He'd told her before that he couldn't tell her about bureau operations, so she didn't ask what he'd be doing. In this case, it was just official business, but he wondered if she ever suspected he was fooling around with some other woman — or doing what he'd begun doing online.

As the shower spray hit his face and warmed his body, he found himself thinking again about Dora. He found he needed to see the nude picture again. Really needed to. Maybe it was being naked.

He shaved quickly, nicking himself slightly under his chin. He half-heartedly toweled his hair dry, combing it back, still a little wet, into his FBI-issue crew cut. He brushed his teeth with about four strokes and put a small piece of toilet paper on the cut. That was all he could manage for his washing up. He shut off the bathroom light and walked toward his den.

He'd dropped his unofficial FBI laptop on his desk when he got home. He popped it open. With a click, he had the picture of Dora in her naughty pose on the screen. Full color. He enjoyed the privacy and safeness of viewing her for a moment. Ogling Dora at the office on a regular basis probably wouldn't be such a good idea. If he got caught, there was the plausible explanation that she was a suspect, but Foster, if he caught him, would probably ask again about Zoot's SAA meetings, which he'd skipped the last couple of days.

On the other hand, there was no way Foster could check on his attendance. Those sessions were confidential. The only way Foster would know he'd backslid on his therapy was if he'd had someone follow him. Not impossible, but unlikely. Zoot erased the image from his screen, closed the laptop and cleansed his mind of such worries. Back to work, he told himself. All in all, it had been a nice interlude, and he'd survived another day without giving up much when it came to urges.

Eventually, Zoot would have to tell Foster what he was finding with the bug in Dora's bedroom. There were hints of insider trading from the conversations he and Urbanski had heard the first day. There were references to a piece of paper being handed over, but there was no proof yet what was on it. Eventually, Dora and her hedge-fund buddy would make a mistake, Zoot was pretty sure. He just needed time, and then he'd break Foster's case for him. With some busts of Victor and his gang in the city, including whatever his computer operation was doing, he could argue to get his old job back. Maybe he'd even be able to nail Dora's dad in the process. That would seal the deal.

One other possibility intrigued him: He had enough evidence to justify interviewing Dora in person. That would be an interesting interrogation. He could sweat her for information. That had been his angry plan for Barnaby at one point, but when he thought about the same tactic for Dora, he got a smile on his face. It was a nice fantasy with him in control. His addiction had been just fantasy up to that point. Nothing face-to-face. Was he ready for the real thing, his own version of that famous happy ending?

* * *

Tesla came over to Barnaby's before her first class, which wasn't until ten that day, a perk of being a senior. She wanted to use his computer for something, she said. But she never got that far.

"Someone copied your hard drive, Mr. G," she whispered after doing her normal security routine.

"How do you know?"

Tesla put her right index finger perpendicular to her lips and said: "Come outside a minute would you?"

Tesla picked up the laptop and walk to the back yard. Once Barnaby had closed the storm door, she said: "I left some traps in case somebody broke in again after the Chinese guys."

"But what would anyone want? I don't have any secrets?"

"Maybe you do but you just don't know it – or maybe someone thinks you do."

Tesla opened the laptop, clicked on an app icon and up popped a video of Urbanski, dated early that morning.

"Look familiar?" she asked Barnaby.

Barnaby's eyes widened.

"He's an FBI agent. I met him this morning."

"He probably searched your house and left a few bugs in there. We should just assume they're listening to whatever we have to say inside."

"But I'm helping them."

"Doesn't look like they trust you." Tesla got a broad grin on her face. "Hope you weren't hiding any illegal drugs or anything,"

Barnaby's body tensed, but he put the gun in the birdhouse out of his head.

Tesla said she'd tell her cyber-security pal that the replacement laptop had been compromised by the bureau.

"In the meantime, that agent might get a few surprises if he tries to open some folders I left on the desktop."

"Your files?"

"No, I store all mine in the cloud so I don't have to worry about hackers – or the police. All they're going to find are viruses."

"There's one surprise that worries me."

"What's that?"

"They may find out we went to Chinatown with a packet of cash and took some customs documents out to the port."

"Nothing illegal in that that we know of."

"It's what we don't know that worries me. The FBI said Victor is a crook, so did we help a crook commit a crime?"

"Let me ask my cyber friend what to do, She's ex-government. Maybe she has some pals who can help."

After Tesla left, Barnaby went out to his backyard again and headed to a shed where he kept some of his birding equipment. In a corner on a high shelf was a dilapidated birdhouse he planned to restore before spring. He pried the roof off it and saw that the pistol Victor had given him was still there. He'd had no plans to use it, but he was happy no one was able to ask him why he didn't have a permit for it. He should have thrown it out, but something had always come up.

* * *

Later that day, Tesla called Veronica. They met at a park not far from Tesla's house. As a couple of dozen Latino men played soccer with grunting intensity in front of them, Tesla explained about the FBI break-in to Barnaby's house.

"Ames and Urbanski were told to lay off Barnaby. We'll have to see what we can do to make their lives a little more unpleasant."

Tesla leaned over and gave Veronica a quick kiss on the cheek.

"Thanks," Tesla said.

"That it?"

"Not exactly."

Tesla told Veronica about their Chinatown and port errands for Victor.

"Could be smuggling or counterfeit goods or both. Doesn't sound like the kind of thing Barnaby would want to get involved with voluntarily."

"He didn't. I was there. We didn't find out about the money or the import documents till we were on our way, when it was sort of too late to back out. And we didn't really have any proof that anything illegal was going on. It just sort of smelled."

Tesla suddenly laughed.

"What?"

"Everyone kept kidding him that I must be his girlfriend, and Mr. G got all flustered."

Veronica flashed a sly smile.

"You're not going all bisexual on me, are you?"

Tesla punched Veronica playfully in the arm.

"Very funny, but, hey, I might. Could improve the dating odds when I go to college."

"So cruel."

"You started it."

"Speaking of school, have you talked to your mom about the NSA offer? Free college and a guaranteed job at the end should sound pretty good."

"Still mulling that over. It's a pretty secret life. You'd be about the only one I could talk to about what I do."

"It's worth it."

"I know the pitch: Cutting-edge equipment. Catch the bad guys. Tons of fun. And make a pile of money later when you go private."

Tesla waited a moment then said; "Can I ask you something?"

"Sure."

"Were you at that hacker meeting by accident the day we met."

Veronica smiled.

"No, but you were a fairly pleasant accident. Speaking of which, I have a little present for you."

Veronica pulled out a new Mac laptop from her carryall bag and handed it to Tesla.

"Wow."

"Maybe you shouldn't use this one with Barnaby's Internet connection. Too many FBI and Chinese agents monitoring that broadband highway."

"You want your replacement laptop back?"

"Leave it. Can't hurt him. At least I hope it won't."

"How'd his own computer turn out?"

"Still transmitting to an captive Internet service provider down in the city."

"Chinese?"

"Looks like Eastern Europeans. Ukrainians, most likely. Robbing bank accounts with stolen sign-ons and IDs And there's an offshoot that's using all the bots to make millions of visits to paying websites. It's an old mob scam, but it pays pretty well."

"You going to arrest them?"

"Hope so. We're not sure exactly where they are. They're using some cutouts in Odessa, but we'll get them eventually and pass what we get onto the FBI cyber unit when we're sure. Brownie points for us and more government contracts."

"Sounds so patriotic."

They both laughed.

"You know," Tesla said. "One of Mr. G's customers has a computer operation above his garment factory down in the city. Wouldn't let us get anywhere near it. We gave him all kinds of good advice on firewalls and such but he didn't seem to be too worried about hackers or passwords."

Veronica gave Tesla her own chaste kiss on the cheek after she got the factory address. She looked at Tesla's face and ran her hand though the right side of her hair.

"You are so delicious."

Tesla smiled back.

"Still jail bait, so watch it."

"I'll restrain myself, but in the meantime don't do anything crazy with any bad guys you run across."

"No worries. To them, I'm just a kid."

*   *   *

Barnaby called the cell number on Zoot's business card and said he was heading into the city to Victor's garment factory. He brought along a tape measure and packed his laptop so he could make some entries in Victor's files. He didn't really need any more information, but he hoped the paraphernalia would give him a ruse to plant the bug. Barnaby explained his plan to Zoot.

"That's good," Zoot said. "Very professional." Zoot was leaning toward regarding Barnaby as just a bumbling hobbyist, but he kept doing things, like coming up with his Victor plan, that made Zoot wonder who was playing whom.

Zoot told Barnaby that he'd drive over to the factory himself and be close enough to test the bug. He said he'd send Barnaby an e-mail from an anonymous account and when the bug was installed, Barnaby should e-mail him that it was done.

"And I'll send you one back that just says, 'Got it.'"

* * *

Victor's foreman Jerzy was surprised to see Barnaby but let him in.

"Mr. Dragon didn't say anything about you coming over."

"I didn't want to bother him. I just need to make a few more measurements before I give him my final report. I got an idea last night, but I'm not sure it will work in this layout. It'll just take a minute."

Before Jerzy could say no, Barnaby put his computer bag down and started making his bogus measurements. He noticed Jerzy had gone over to a wall phone and was making a call, probably to Victor, Barnaby guessed. Not wanting to be told to leave before his mission was complete, Barnaby went over to Jerzy and whispered, "I need to use your office phone for a call. I left my cell in its charger this morning."

Jerzy told the person on the other end of the line: "Just a minute." He followed Barnaby into the factory office. He scanned the papers on the top of his desk and grabbed two folders.

"Make it snappy," he said. "I got things to do in here."

As Jerzy walked out of the office, Barnaby withdrew the bug box from his jacket hip pocket and quickly stripped the protective paper from the device's bottom. With the bug in his left hand, he used his right to call his home phone to see if there were any messages on his answering machine. The phone rang and Barnaby punched in the remote access code. As he heard the familiar recording voice say that he had one message waiting. As he did, he leaned forward and planted the bug as far back under the drawer as he could. He pressed hard in an upward fashion to make sure the adhesive was as effective as possible.

It was done, and he breathed a sigh of relief. But that didn't last long. Panic set in when he realized his fingerprints were on the device. Victor would know it was him if Jerzy found the bug.

He looked out to the factory floor and saw Jerzy's searing eyes were trained on him. While still on the phone, he tried to act casually in grabbing some tissues from a box on Jerzy's desk. He put the elbow of his phone arm on the desk and stretched his other arm underneath it till he found the exposed side of the device. He wiped it as thoroughly as he could, hoping he wouldn't jar the bug loose or put it out of commission.

Once done, he stuffed the tissues in his jacket picket and pushed the number 5 on Jerzy's phone to finally get the voice-mail message. It was from Barbara. In a weak voice, she said she was in the hospital and just wanted him to know so he wouldn't be worried if he came by her house and found it empty.

Not worried would have been his state of mind if he hadn't gotten the call, but suddenly it was one more thing to tie his stomach in knots. He was concerned about her as a friend, but he was also wondering if she'd be able to do the Christmas work for the caring committee. He hoped she would not ask him to fill in. He had too many other things going on in his life, many of which he would prefer to eliminate if only he could.

Barnaby hung up the phone and said to no one in particular "Testing, testing." Not sure what else to do, he opened his computer and installed the cell device that let him use the Internet no matter where he was in the New York area — a smart purchase Tesla had recommended. He clicked his browser and went to his e-mail site, which was run by his cable TV company. He saw the message from Zoot's alias. It said Howdy! in the subject line. Barnaby responded with "Done." and waited. He wasn't sure what he'd do if the reply wasn't "Got it." He didn't know anything about how the bug worked. And he didn't have a backup. Was he supposed to move it to a better reception location? He and Zoot hadn't discussed that. Barnaby stared at his e-mail screen as nothing happened for almost a minute. Jerzy was watching him from the wall phone location, chatting again. He hung up the phone and headed toward Barnaby. Just before he arrived, Zoot's message appeared, and Barnaby closed his computer before Jerzy arrived.

"All done," Barnaby said. "Be in touch."

Barnaby put out is hand. Jerzy gave him an unenthusiastic shake and said nothing.

Barnaby left the factory and headed for the street, wondering if he could spot Zoot. He walked around the block looking in car windows and noticing a couple of parked vans, but he chose not to knock on their back doors in case Jerzy had sent someone to follow him.

In a van two blocks from Victor's factory, Zoot and Urbanski, headphones on, listened to the ambient noise of the manager's office until they finally heard footsteps on the bare wood floor.

"Showtime," Urbanski said.

Jerzy picked up the phone, checked the call log and punched in a number. Victor Dragon answered on the other end.

"Looks like he called himself, if that makes any sense," Jerzy said.

"Maybe someone there or he was picking up his messages. You said he left his cell at home, right?"

"Yeah. Bit of a goof if you ask me."

"I still think he's harmless, and he's given me some ideas to save some dough. Plus I got a little plan for him, so leave him alone for now. But keep an eye on him. And let me know if he shows up unannounced again."

"Gotcha."

"By the way, what time is Lin coming over there?"

Jerzy checked his watch.

"About 15 minutes. I got the latest designs for him. He says he's got some new targets."

"Good. And one other thing. I need you to run a plate for me with your source in the DMV. Kristal Power had a strange dude visit her at home. She had a bad feeling about it, so let me know whose car it is."

* * *

John Lin entered the vast garment building and took the elevator to a floor two above the one for Victor's factory. He got out with another man who walked into an office almost in front of the elevator door. Making sure the hallway was empty, Lin walked to the southern stairway exit door and went down two floors to Victor's place. The hallway was empty and he buzzed for entry, watching to see if anyone appeared in the hall before he got in. Jerzy let Lin in and escorted him back to the manager's office as half a dozen Latino workers busied themselves with piecework at tables on the floor. After handshakes, Jerzy handed over an envelope.

"Latest Dior and Calvin Klein in there. They'll be in Penny's and Macy's in time for Christmas, so you'll need to hurry."

Lin smiled.

"We'll have something for the tourists before then. Worldwide, we'll make millions on these."

"Usual financial arrangement?"

"Yes. You should see the money in your account by the end of the day after I check these out."

"There shouldn't be anything to check. They come right out of the safe."

"You know, if you guys ever decide to expand to Silicon Valley, we should talk. I have some safes at Apple and Intel I'd like you to break into."

"High-tech. That could be cool."

Lin handed over his own envelope.

"Those are some hot designers who could be big shortly. We need to see what they're up to."

From the surveillance van, Urbanski said: "You think that's our Mr. Lin?"

"I'd say that's pretty certain even though Lin's a pretty common name. Let's roll the truck over to the front entrance and see what we see. I'll take the front; you go over to the side."

Ten minutes later, Urbanski saw Lin come out of the side entrance and snapped his photo with his telephone lens from inside a nearby coffee shop.

"Hello, John," he said to himself.

*　*　*

Barnaby visited Barbara at the hospital late that afternoon. He was almost happy to see that visiting hours would be over 45 minutes. He wanted to pay his respects, but he didn't want to get dragged any more into Barbara's painful life than he had been. He bought her a small flowering plant at the gift shop. There was no label. Begonias, he guessed. Gwyn was the expert on plants.

Barbara was hooked up to an IV drip and looked dreadfully gray. She managed a slight smile while wincing in obvious pain as she tried to sit up straighter for her guest.

"I had a bit of an episode," she said, "so they brought me in."

"You'll be going home soon, I hope."

"If I'm lucky, it won't be feet first."

"Don't joke like that."

"Jokes are about all I have these days. Them and my sister – and you."

"I forgot you had a sister."

"No surprise. She's out in the boonies in Montana. Can't afford plane tickets to visit very often. When I go, at least she won't have to feel guilty about that."

"You're not going anywhere. You'll be on you feet in no time."

"I doubt it, and with all the caring committee work to do, I'm not sure what will happen to those poor people counting on us."

"I'll see if I can pitch in."

"If you could, call Sadie Tucker. She knows the drill. She doesn't think she has the skills to run the whole show, but I think she does."

"OK. But just as a precaution."

"My doctor wants to put me in a hospice. To me that's just a long-term death watch. It'll be just lingering pain and painkillers. I won't even know if I'm alive."

"What about treatment?"

"Way too late for that. I always had something else to do. The caring committee or my garden or some silly excuse. Now I'm in the soup, and the cannibals are all around the pot, licking their chops over my sorry carcass."

She tried to laugh but wound up coughing again.

"I'm sure something will come up," Barnaby said. "They're finding new cures all the time."

"I'm not counting on that, but I do have a plan. It's not final yet. I want to think about it. When I get home, would you come over and hear me out?"

"Of course, and I'll give you an honest reaction to whatever it is."

Chapter 19

With the new bug in place, Zoot and Urbanski monitored the conversations from the garment factory for a week. Barnaby took the opportunity to visit a couple of Angelo's other clients and wrote up his formal reports for Victor on how to streamline his fish operation and his garment factory. By Thursday afternoon, Barnaby had proofread them and called Victor for an appointment. Victor chose Monday, saying he was getting out of the city early for the weekend. Shortly after the conversation, Barnaby got a visit from Zoot.

"Hear you're talking to Victor on Monday."

"But how," Barnaby said, his words trailing off.

"You have no secrets from me."

"I'm not sure I like this arrangement. I was willing to help the bureau, but this seems to be crossing a line for just an average citizen. I expect a little more privacy."

Zoot laughed.

"Average citizen. Barnaby, you are not within a light year of average. You are way over there in the kook galaxy."

"I don't see..."

"Paling around with Chinese counterfeiters, Ukrainian mobsters and hottie school girls at a Harlem whorehouse. Not what I'd call average. But, hey, I'm not complaining. I couldn't have dreamed up an inside man like you in a million years, and now that I've got you, I'm not giving you up."

"This isn't what I signed up for. I was just going to be a deputy."

"Hey, if you don't want to help, I know a friendly federal prosecutor who can persuade a grand jury that you are one of Victor's co-conspirators. Even if you beat the rap, you'll spend your life savings doing it, so just shut up and do what you're told."

Barnaby felt a swelling anger toward Zoot. It was an unusual sensation for him. There weren't many people or things in life he disliked.

"Don't be nervous," Zoot said. "It's not like we're asking you to shoot anyone."

Barnaby thought of the gun Victor had given him and entertained a brief fantasy of shooting Zoot, just as he had with the Canada geese. When he stopped to think rationally about the idea, though, killing anyone or anything seemed so far from what he thought he was capable of, he put the idea out of his mind and resolved to get rid of Victor's weapon as soon as he could. It was silly to hold on to it. Even if his Chinese attackers came back, he'd hardly be able to run out to his backyard shed to retrieve it in time from its bird-house hiding place.

His Chinese attackers were just a few hundred yards away in their van, and saw Zoot leave Barnaby's house.

"His place is like Grand Central," Mr. Bo said. "How am I supposed to kill him with no one noticing?"

"Looks like this won't be the day, but soon," Mr. Xi said. "Very soon."

* * *

On Saturday, Barbara called after breakfast to say she'd checked herself out of the hospital and needed to talk to him about her plan to deal with her illness. Barnaby was there by ten and found the side door open a crack. Barbara was in bed in her nightgown and robe under her quilted duvet. She was sitting up with two fat pillows behind her. She told Barnaby to take a seat on the foot of the bed. Barnaby sat on the corner. Barbara twinged in pain as the mattress gave way when Barnaby sat on it. He jumped up to stop her discomfort.

"Sit down, sit down. It wasn't you. These things are coming in cycles. If they keep going like this, it will become just one continuous pain."

"I'm so sorry."

Barbara let out a long sigh.

"Christ, if I knew I'd just die, I'd let it happen, and everything would be over, but apparently I'm just headed for seas of pain — not a nice, quick painful end. That's what I wanted to talk to you about. I want something faster."

Barnaby knew all too well about lingering pain. Gwyn had been through it at the end but there had been a merciful out for her. They'd decided together that it was best to pull the plug on the life-support machine, and they had. It was a hardest thing he'd ever had to do, but, in the end, it was also the smart one.

"I have a way to stop the pain," Barbara continued, "and it will also help my sister."

Barnaby wasn't sure where Barbara was going with her idea and kept silent as she laid out the details of what she had in mind.

"My sister is pretty hard up. I send her some money from Social Security when I can, which isn't often enough. We're both in a bad way financially — in income terms anyway. I have some assets. My house is paid off and I have a little in my 401(k). And I have some insurance."

"Whole life can be a good investment," Barnaby said, trying to stay upbeat.

"It's not whole life. She doesn't get anything unless I'm dead, which may take too long to be of any use to her if I leave things up to nature."

"Is there some emergency?"

"Yeah. She just found out she needs an operation pretty fast, and her crummy insurance plan won't cover most of it."

"What about Obamacare?"

"She never signed up for it. Stupid, but that's my darling sister."

"That doesn't sound good."

"No. But if I died, she'd get the insurance money. She could get the operation, and the cash would help her daughter, too, who's not in great health either."

"That's terrible."

"Yeah. She just lost her job. They got their own little soap opera going."

Barbara suddenly had another pain seizure.

"Is there anything I can do? Get you a pill or something?"

Barbara put up her hand to indicate that wouldn't be necessary. She composed herself, took a deep breath and finally said: "Could you get me a gun?"

Barnaby's eyes blinked.

"A gun?"

"Yes. That's my plan to make everything better."

"I don't see..."

"I'm going to shoot myself and end it all – and let my sister get the insurance money."

"You can't do that!"

"There isn't any other way. I've thought a lot about it. I'm in for a long painful slog. I won't die for a long time, and if I take enough drugs to deal with the pain, I'll just be among the walking dead. A zombie. So why not get it over with and get her some money while she can use it?"

"But shooting yourself?"

"It's the sensible thing."

"It doesn't make much sense to me."

"Maybe not, but I'd still need your help — and not just in getting the gun."

"I don't see how I."

Barbara interrupted.

"Hear me out."

Barnaby just nodded his head.

"The thing is, it can't look like suicide. There's a provision in the policy that disqualifies my death if I take my own life, so it has to look like murder. In fact, my sister gets more if I'm murdered."

"How will you arrange that?"

Barbara coughed several times and finally said: "I'm going to shoot myself and then you take away the gun and some of my things."

"Me?"

"Yes. So it looks like a burglary."

"But that's a crime."

"It's just assisted suicide. If Dr. Kevorkian were still alive, I'd ask him to bring a gun, but you're the only one I know who could do it."

"Barbara, I, I just don't know...."

"Just don't say no. Think about it. In the meantime, could you get a gun? You know, go to Pennsylvania or one of those hunting states?"

"I don't see how that helps. I'd have to show an ID and the bullet would come back to me — and you — and I'd have to explain or go to prison. And your sister would get nothing once I said it was a suicide."

Barbara began to sniffle after Barnaby's reality check. Perhaps out of desperation she asked: "You know any crooks who could get one? You know, on the QT?"

Barnaby's mind tossed up the image of the gun in the birdhouse.

"Maybe."

Barbara managed her broadest smile of the day.

"That would be wonderful."

"I can't guarantee anything. And it might take a little time."

"Come back Saturday, and we'll see where we are, OK? I'll call to remind you."

Barnaby thought about Zoot's ability to listen in on his calls

"Don't call. I'll remember."

* * *

Zoot and Urbanski, having learned John Lin was coming back to Victor's garment factory on Monday morning, arranged for a squad of six agents from the counterfeit goods unit to accompany them on a raid to seize the stolen clothing designs and arrest anyone at the factory. Shortly after ten, Lin was spotted entering the side entrance to the building. An agent posing as the freight elevator operator was surprised to see him call for a floor two above Victor's factory.

"Pirate10 out on four, the agent radioed to the rest of the squad. "Guess he's walking down to the factory."

A hastily installed video camera on the factory floor, showed Lin dressed in a tailored charcoal gray, two-button suit, a few minutes later. He buzzed for entry. Once he was in, the agents raced to the entrance. Victor had his own video trained on the door, so Special Agent James Dolan had dressed in a delivery uniform to deal with that problem. He pressed the factory-door buzzer. When Jerzy came on the intercom, Dolan said: "Delivery."

"Leave it there," Jerzy said.

"Need a signature," Dolan said, a cardboard roll in one hand and a clipboard on the other. "Looks like some plans or something."

Victor's manager came to the door and cracked it open carefully. Dolan handed him the clipboard with the delivery receipt form on top. As soon as the manager had the board in one hand, Agent Urbanski kicked open the door and pulled his service pistol.

"FBI," Urbanski said calmly. "Move back and shut up. Grip that clipboard with both hands and let's walk back to the office. No fast moves or I might think my life's in danger."

Jerzy looked hesitant about what to do.

"Don't play hero," Dolan added. "Counterfeit goods aren't worth losing your life over."

Jerzy did as he was told. Dolan, who'd been followed by Zoot and the rest of the team, found John Lin sitting impatiently in the office.

"I'm guessing we're going to find some very interesting designs somewhere in here, so no one move while we conduct a little search," Zoot said.

Lin's eyes widened at the announcement.

"I have diplomatic immunity," he said, his voice showing no fear or other emotion.

"Really? Well, before I can verify what you say, you'll have to come with us. The local federal jail has all the comforts of home. Water, electricity and stuff that passes for food. You'll be well cared for as we verify your status and ask a few questions about why a diplomat is involved in criminal activity."

"I know nothing about any crime."

"You were just here to order a dress or something?"

"I don't have to say anything."

"You already have," Urbanski said. "And we have it all on tape."

Two of the agents searched the office and found the plans Lin had ordered up in an envelope on the manager's desk.

"Glad we didn't have to blow a safe or anything to get these," Zoot said, noting an open safe.

"Put everything in an evidence bag," Zoot told the agent who'd squatted down to do a search. "Maybe we'll find something with Victor's name on it."

"Who's Victor?" Jerzy asked.

"That would be your boss."

"I'm the only boss here."

Zoot shrugged.

"If you're willing to take the hit, fine. Victor is into so much stuff, we'll get him eventually. In the meantime, this will be a nice little dent in his annual revenue, and I'm guessing you guys will be radioactive with the Chinese for a while."

The agents put the manager and Lin in handcuffs. About a dozen Latino workers were huddled in a corner.

"What do we do with them?" Dolan asked.

"Nothing. Unless one of them has info on Victor, which I doubt. If they all clam up, tell them to go home, wherever that is. If we haul them in we'll be doing paper work till January."

*   *   *

In the lobby, Zoot and his team ran into Foster and a squad from the New York office's cybercrime unit.

"What you doing here, Zoot?" Foster asked.

"Counterfeit goods bust...with a Chinese government connection."

"Nice. We're doing Eastern Europeans. Boiler-room operation up on eight. They set up a network of slave computers to drain bank accounts and rip off website operators."

Zoot nodded silently, sensing Foster's triumph might not be total good news.

"Probably all techno gobbledygook to you, but there is an organized crime angle."

"What's that?"

"Local mobster teamed up with some guys in the Ukraine, where we can't get the locals to do anything about them."

"So who was upstairs?"

"Bunch of geeks hired by some mystery man. Word is it's one of Victor Dragon's operations, but we haven't got proof yet."

"Victor Dragon?"

"Yeah, you probably remember him from your days on our unit. Minor guy back then, but seems to have stepped up."

"Yeah, I remember him," Zoot said, his eyes closed to slits. "Like I heard about him yesterday."

Chapter 20

While the FBI raids were going on, Barnaby kept this appointment with Victor, arriving about eleven. He laid out his plans for the fish operation and the factory. Victor looked over the blueprints and the memos and said he was pleased. He put the materials aside and told Barnaby he might have some other businesses for him to look at.

"We might even be able to go partners on something," Victor said.

Before Barnaby could respond to the surprise offer, Victor's phone rang. Victor listened to the caller for a while and his face turned angry.

"The fuck you mean both places? That's impossible."

Victor nodded as he listened to the person on the other end of the line.

"Well, bail them out best you can, and remind them to keep their freakin' mouths shut."

"Difficulties?" Barnaby asked when the call was over.

"Appears I got a rat problem at the factory. Gonna need an exterminator."

* * *

Late that afternoon, Tesla, just home from school, got a visit from Veronica, who'd slipped her slim, six-foot body into red leather pants and a matching jacket over a black silk blouse.

Tesla had on black jeans and T-shirt with an orange ideograph on it.

"That's nice looking," Veronica said, pointing to the Chinese character. "What's it mean?"

"Well when I bought it in the city, the guy said it was the symbol for freedom, but a Chinese friend of mine at school said it means stinky foreigner, which I sort of like even better."

"Can't trust the Chinese."

"So it seems."

"Speaking of hackers, you had a good guess on that place in the Garment District. With a little assist, the FBI rolled up the botnet operation. Everybody except the guys in the Ukraine, and maybe the big boss here. But at least they shut them down. You friend's computer should be OK once we deactivate the slave orders."

Veronica handed over Barnaby's original laptop.

"One other thing," Veronica said.

Veronica pulled out an envelope from her briefcase and handed it to Tesla.

"Full ride to Stanford if you want it – with a little public service due at the end. There's a monthly stipend to sweeten things while you attend. And a little signing bonus.

Tesla looked at the letter, which said she'd been accepted for the spring term.

"Spring? I haven't even graduated from high school."

"No sweat. We can make arrangements for you to get credit in California while you get started. You'll miss the prom, but I'm guessing that's not a deal killer."

Tesla smiled.

"Not really. Bad demographics."

"Well, let me know...I take it you'll want to talk it over with your mom."

"Yeah, but she'll be cool. It'll free up some money. It's more my call. Mr. G. may be a bit at loose ends, though."

"That's why God invented e-mail and Skype video calls. You can still be his IT manager, if you want."

"Guess I can't tell him what's going on."

"Definitely not. And nothing to the FBI if that Zoot guy comes snooping around. You're just a high school student who likes reptiles."

*   *   *

That evening, Tesla went over to Barnaby's and returned his laptop. She wiped the hard drive clean and downloaded his photos and other files from the cloud server.

"Should be good as new, but be careful about opening strange e-mails. They're full of viruses, and I might not always be around to watch your back."

"Well, we have at least till graduation. More than half a year."

Tesla crinkled her eyes.

"Not really. I'm starting early. At Stanford."

"Stanford! That's tremendous. Your mother must be thrilled."

"Haven't told her yet. Just found out."

"I feel honored to be the first to know."

"Couldn't have done it without you, Mr. G."

She gave him a hug, which flustered Barnaby for a moment.

"It was I who couldn't have done it without you. Those early computers would have been just doorstops to me."

"I'll still be around online to help out. I'll send you my new e-mail when I get settled. Just shoot me a note if you have a problem."

"Don't worry about me. I can take care of myself."

*   *   *

With Victor in limbo that week fending off grand-jury sub-poenas, Barnaby called Angelo to see if any of his other accounting clients might have need of his services. Angelo gave him two leads, but he was elusive when Barnaby pressed for details about whether Victor needed any follow-up visits to implement his advice on the fish warehouse and the garment factory.

"He's little preoccupied just now, Barnaby. I'd leave him alone till you get a call."

John Lin had also been occupied sorting out his diplomatic immunity claim with the FBI. The bureau had had his house in Sleepy Hollow under surveillance, so he was reluctant to go to the Canal Street store or to try to give them the slip on a trip to his hide-away office in the city. He decided his only safe bet was to visit the consulate to bring First Secretary Wong into the picture on Barnaby.

"I don't think it's a coincidence they arrested me after that idiot Gilbert visited Victor's factory."

"What does Victor think?"

"Haven't been able to ask him since the arrests. Seems to think the guy is OK. Got some special plans for him. Doesn't make that much sense to me. I'd just as soon kill him."

"All Right. Give the go-ahead to Bo and Xi then."

"And if he turns out to be FBI?"

"It's a stolen sniper gun, so they shouldn't be able to trace it to us."

"Where'd we get it?"

"A New York City police department locker."

Lin laughed.

"That should complicate things nicely."

*   *   *

Barnaby had Friday free and went birding at the point both at dawn and late afternoon. He saw a sign near the parking lot saying "Puppy Lost." There was a picture of a cute Dalmatian puppy on the photocopied flyer, which was stapled to a wooden post. On the walk back from the extreme end of the point, Barnaby spotted a dark shape in a leafless tree on the south side of the peninsula. He brought his spotter into focus and spied a male bald eagle sitting in a roost on a thick gray branch. His first reaction was one of happiness that the eagles had finally returned to the area for cold season. But his mood quickly turned black. On closer inspect he saw the huge bird was picking at a small white and black carcass. Barnaby knew it was not a fish or duck.

As he reflected on his sighting on the way back to his car, Barnaby saw the puppy sign again. There was a phone number in big type at the bottom. It was a call he would not make, and in reversed circumstances, would not want to receive. Better the fantasy of a loving new home than that cold shower of Darwinian reality.

* * *

That Saturday, Barnaby lingered over coffee and toast after getting up. He hadn't fully made up his mind whether to help Barbara, but he retrieved the gun Victor had given him from the broken birdhouse in the shed. With the gun in his trunk, he parked his car in a village lot and did some shopping. He returned to his vehicle and put his purchases in the trunk. He emptied one bag and put the towel-wrapped weapon in it.

He walked with the bag to Barbara's, going around the block a couple of times to make sure he wasn't followed. Barbara was in bed again, her eyes closed as her voice rattled in pain. Beside her bed on the floor was some gold jewelry, her cell phone and her wallet with some cash sticking out. Her jewelry chest and a small gray security box were nearby, their lids opened. The boxes looked as if their contents had been rifled. Some certificates of deposit were on the floor.

Barnaby called out Barbara's name again from her bedroom doorway.

"Is that you, Barnaby?" she asked.

"Yes," he said softly.

"Did you have any luck?"

Barnaby knew exactly what she meant and slowly took the towel and its contents from the plastic bag. He unwrapped it and showed the taped pistol to Barbara.

"Is it loaded?"

Barnaby realized he hadn't bothered to check and discovered it was not. He took out the handful of bullets he had in his parka pocket and, careful not to touch the slug end, loaded the gun, a .32-caliber automatic that took six in the magazine and one in the chamber. He handed the weapon to Barbara, who barely had the strength to hold it. She seized up again in pain, and her left arm went limp on the bed covers as the weight of the weapon pulled it down.

"When do you plan to do it?"

Barbara labored to breathe but finally said, "I think now. Everything is ready for you to take, and I don't think I can stand another night."

"But I'm not ready."

"You'll have to be."

Barbara drew the pistol toward her head, then stopped.

"Is it noisy?"

The question made Barnaby pause. "I don't know," he said. "I've never fired it."

"Where did you get it?"

"A friend."

"Won't it be traced if the police have the bullet?"

"Not this friend," Barnaby said, making a more honest assessment of Victor Dragon than he'd done before.

"Maybe I should use a pillow to deaden the sound."

"You might suffocate."

Barbara laughed painfully at Barnaby's remark.

"That's the least of my worries."

Barnaby looked at the pillow.

"You know, maybe you should just suffocate yourself."

Barbara shook her head.

"I think that would be even more painful, and I don't think I could keep it up till the end."

"A burglar might try that instead of a gun. Just to be quieter."

"My neighbors are away, so I don't think that's much of a problem."

Barbara slid down in the bed and reached for a pillow on the other side, pulling to her chest.

"After I'm gone, just take the gun and those things on the floor. You can use one of my pillowcases to carry them. Then get rid of everything somehow." Barbara went on another coughing jag before she could add: "Better wipe the door handles on your way out. I wiped most other surfaces down with a sponge."

"Very thorough," Barnaby said, thinking that Barbara had watched too many detective shows on TV.

"And if anyone does ask you about being in the house, just tell the truth — at least the truth up till now. Say you were giving me a hand with the presents for the poor. You weren't the only one, so you'll have good cover."

"I'm sorry we couldn't have robbed a bank together," Barnaby joked, trying to break the tension of the moment.

"Maybe in another life."

Barbara asked Barnaby to put the pillow lightly over her head. After he had, she slowly cocked her left arm so that the muzzle of the pistol was about where her temple was. She pressed the gun further inward so that it created a dimple in the pillow. Barnaby prepared for the worst, rooting at the last minute for a quiet shot so he wouldn't have to explain himself to a neighbor.

Before anything had happened, he turned around and walked toward the bedroom door. Barbara lifted one corner of the pillow with her right hand.

"Don't leave."

"I'm just closing the door. To keep things quiet."

"OK."

Her voice sounded like a wheeze.

Barbara put the pillow corner back down and pressed the pistol again to her temple. Barnaby held his breath waiting for the sound of the shot. He wondered if it was too late to talk Barbara out of her plan. After about 30 seconds, she lifted the pillow corner again and said, "I can't do it."

Barnaby let out a sigh of relief.

"I'm glad. So very glad."

Barbara let out a sigh of exasperation.

"No. I mean I can't pull the trigger." Barbara pulled the pillow off. "On top of everything else, I have arthritis in my left hand, and the trigger just won't budge. You have to help me."

"I, I can't."

"You must. Mine will be the hand on the trigger, so don't fret about that. You'll just be giving me a little boost."

Barbara put the pillow over her head again and repositioned the pistol. After Barnaby did nothing for a few seconds, she lifted the pillow corner again and just said, in a pleading tone, "Barnaby!"

Barnaby moved closer to the bed. Only after he heard another cry of pain from Barbara did he put his trigger finger on top of hers. He could feel her feeble attempts to get the job done. He still hesitated. Unable to suppress a painful memory of his wife on her final day of pain did his finger move. It wasn't really something he did voluntarily. In his mind he was watching the doctor flip the off switch on the life support system, and when he saw and heard that happen, his finger on the trigger moved.

He heard a muffled pop and felt Barbara's hand slip from the trigger guard. He found he was holding the pistol on his own. He gamely put the weapon back into his parka pocket and jammed the kitchen towel in too. He waited a few moments, not sure if the bullet had done its job. Barbara didn't move. He reached for her left hand and checked for a pulse. He didn't feel one, but he wasn't sure if he'd done it properly. He put his right ear on her left breast to see if he could hear a heartbeat. He couldn't. He didn't want to lift the pillow from her head. There was a hole in it with gunpowder around it, and a few feathers from inside had shot out after he and Barbara had pulled the trigger. He couldn't bring himself to look at her face.

He decided that if she were dead, that was it. If she weren't, she might be shortly, and the deed would have been done to her satisfaction. If she somehow survived, she'd be taken to a hospital and they would have to see what else could be done, given the new situation. Nothing for him to do but go away.

Almost mechanically he loaded the jewelry, wallet and other things into a pillowcase he found in a chest at the foot of Barbara's bed. He decided he couldn't touch either the pillow with the bullet hole or the one under her head. He looked back at the sight of Barbara lying prone and still before he left the bedroom. Had he done a horrible thing? Was he now a murderer? Barbara said it was assisted suicide. He would cling to that if ever asked, but he hoped he would be the only one to ask any questions.

At the kitchen door, he spotted a recyclable cloth shopping bag with the name of a village farmer's market on it. It occurred to him that it was not the most natural thing in the world to be walking down a village street with a pillowcase full of god-knows-what. He stuffed the case's swag into the green bag and went out the door, wiping the handles with the edges of the pillowcase, as Barbara had instructed. He stowed the case in the bag, too.

He saw no one on the street. Barnaby retraced his steps to his car. He found he'd been given a ticket because the meter had expired. That might prove a good thing because it would show he was away from Barbara's, doing some shopping. He put the bag with Barbara's things in his trunk and went off to a nearby drugstore to purchase some toiletries he didn't really need. He ignored his normal cash-only rule and used a credit card, which would record a time stamp. It wasn't the perfect alibi, but it was the start of one, especially if Barbara hadn't died straight away.

Barnaby drove to the point. He parked in the upper lot. He walked through the campgrounds. All but the most stalwart RV campers had moved on. He passed one dog walker and her gray-muzzled Golden retriever. He said "Afternoon," and she nodded in return. He made his way to the rock beach on the west side of the landmass. He took out the pistol and wiped off the trigger to remove Barbara's fingerprint. He took the pistol by its taped handle and tossed it as hard as he could into the river, hearing the kerplunk just after he spotted the little splash a moment later. Light's faster than sound, he reminded himself, not sure why that science-class lesson had surfaced at that moment.

He decided he shouldn't toss Barbara's things in the river. A burglar wouldn't have. He could ditch the wallet in a trashcan after taking the cash and the credit cards out. That would seem right to the police. Then he decided it would be better to use some public incinerator to get rid of everything. There was one in Peekskill, he remembered. But on the way, he turned off on a road to a quarry just north of his village. In the summertime, kids swam in the inky water that filled it, ignoring the "Danger! No Swimming" signs. Local legend was that it was bottomless. As Barnaby emptied the contents of the pillowcase into the quarry from the ridge above it, he hoped it would be deep enough.

With his tracks covered, the enormity of what had happened finally hit him as he drove home. The moisture in his eyes welled up from somewhere deep inside him. By the time he'd gone about a mile, the tears flowed. His gentle sobs propelled the liquid drops down his face toward his mouth. Involuntarily he licked the edges of his lips and tasted the saltiness that had been in his body just minutes before. He was not an emotional person normally. He regarded himself as a businessman who relied on logic more than emotion, but he found the tears an unexpected gift, just as he had the day Gwyn had died.

Down Barnaby's block, Mr. Bo and Mr. Xi were finally back on duty with Lin's new orders, having been pulled off at the last minute from another assignment at the port in New Jersey.

"Wake up," Xi said. "He's back."

Bo was startled out of a light slumber.

"Shit! I could have had a shot."

"No worries. Let's get it right. It's not about speed."

"Wonder where he's been?"

"Don't really care. We know where he is. That's all we need." Mr. Bo checked the sniper's rifle on his lap one more time.

"Past is past. We'll just nail him when he comes out."

"Frontal shot is best."

"Heart or head?"

"Head. At this distance, heart can be tricky."

A tap of a police baton on Xi's driver-side window interrupted the conversation. A fit black man dressed in a Neighborhood Watch vest and snakeskin cowboy boots signaled with a twirling motion of his free hand for Mr. Xi to roll down his tinted window.

"Get that rifle out of sight!" Xi whispered to Bo. "If we're lucky the windows are so dark, he won't have seen it."

"It's four feet long!"

"Do what you can, and hurry up."

Bo put the weapon between his legs and covered the stock with the lined trench coat that had been lying across this lap to keep him warm. With the rifle essentially useless as a weapon, he put his right hand inside his suit jacket, stationing it close to the Glock in his shoulder holster.

Xi, seeing that things were in order, finally lowered the power window and offered a confident "Yes?"

"Hi there. Vernon with Neighborhood Watch. We were just noticing you guys have been sitting here for a while, and we did a little checking, and it does not seem you are from around here."

"Yes?"

"Well, we just wanted to make sure nothing bad was going on. You know there's a lot of crime these days, and Sing Sing prison is just over there, so, you know, we neighbors are just being careful."

Mr. Xi just nodded.

"You visiting anyone in the neighborhood?" Vernon asked.

Unable to say they knew Barnaby Gilbert, Xi just said: "No. We just stopped to take a little nap. We were on a long drive from upstate, and this looked like a quiet place."

"Where you headed?"

"Back to the city."

"Huh."

Vernon didn't say anything for a while, and finally Xi asked: "Will that be all?"

"I guess...except for one thing. You guys weren't coming back from hunting or something like that? You know, from up-state."

Xi looked confused at the question.

"No. Nothing like that," he said.

"Well the reason I ask is that rifle under your partner's coat."

Bo started to grab his Glock pistol when the glass on his side of the vehicle shattered as a steel rifle butt came through it. Vernon pressed a button on the end of his nightstick and a thin, sharp blade shot out the other end. The tip of the blade wound up against Xi's jugular vein about the same time a rifle muzzle was placed against Bo's right temple by the man who had shattered the window.

"Now here is how this is going to work," Vernon said. "Your partner is going to grab the end of his rifle stock with his right hand and gently hand it to my partner over there. And then any other weapons like, maybe a switchblade or a pistol in a shoulder holster. All very carefully. In the meantime, my guy will keep his finger on his trigger until he gets everything from you guys, and if all goes well, I won't have to put this blade through your neck. Understood?"

"We have diplomatic immunity," Xi said.

"Now that is the second time someone who looks Chinese has said that to a federal officer in the New York area this week...You know a guy named John Lin?"

Xi's eyes blinked. Bo just continued making the weapons transfers.

"You must know him. Tall guy. Nice dresser. Designer-type stuff. Looks a little like a tall Jackie Chan."

"I don't think so."

"Well, lotta Chinese around these days, even in the consulate, I suppose. Anyway, he made the same claim, and it only took a couple of days before we were able to release him, so you should be out in about the same time if what you say is true."

"Out?"

"Yes, I'm afraid you will be the guests of the United States of America at a little facility down in the city we call the MCC. It's pretty much a federal jail, but there are lots of interesting people down there. They know about guns and knives and meth and all sorts of things you guys may have in common."

"You're not with Neighborhood Watch, I take it," Xi said.

Vernon took out a small digital recorder from his side jacket pocket, hit a button and out came the last few seconds of Xi talking to Bo about Barnaby Gilbert.

"Not exactly."

Chapter 21

The Westchester County newspaper had the story of Barbara's death in its Monday edition under the headline: "Woman Killed During Home Invasion." The story was short and quoted unidentified police officials who said Barbara had been killed with a small-caliber weapon during an apparent daylight robbery of her home. It said police were seeking further information from neighbors or other parties about the crime. The end of the story said Barbara had a sister in Montana who was next of kin.

On Wednesday, there was a death notice in the paper that highlighted Barbara's caring-committee work. It said there would be a wake at a local funeral home on Friday with the burial on Saturday at a nearby cemetery.

Barnaby went to the wake, a closed-casket affair. He spotted a woman he assumed was Barbara's sister at the head of the reception line. She had a young woman at her side. Barnaby was about to sign the guest book but decided at the last minute not to. He introduced himself to the woman and said he'd worked with Barbara on the caring committee. Her sister, whose name was Ellen, thanked him for coming.

"She was a good friend of my wife's," Barnaby said. "A wonderful person. She helped a lot of people."

"I met some of them already. There have been about a hundred who came. I had no idea."

"She was very fond of you too."

"She mentioned me?"

"Of course."

"I don't know what I'll do without her. She always gave me a little something to tide me over. Times have been tough."

Barnaby hesitated before his next remark then finally said, "If there is a silver lining in this, I think you'll find she provided for you and your daughter."

"I haven't had time to think about that yet."

"There's her house, of course. I'm guessing she left it to you in her will."

"She had a will?"

"Pretty sure. There may be a copy in her house. If not there, she banked at Chase, so maybe there's a safe deposit box at the local branch. Check that. I used to see her there on occasion."

"That would be a godsend."

"I think the house is paid for. You can sell it or move in if you want to leave Montana."

Ellen looked at the floor at the suggestion, then brought her head up.

"I don't know."

"And I think she had some insurance. You should look into that."

"Do you know which company?"

Barnaby realized he didn't. He was unprepared for the situation in so many ways. What if Barbara's sister couldn't find the insurance details. Would all the plotting have been for nothing?

"No," he said. "But check the house. There may be a lock box or something in there. That's what I have. Maybe in her bedroom closet."

In the parking lot of the funeral home, Barnaby found Zoot waiting for him and tensed up when Zoot asked: "Friend of yours?"

"What are you doing here?" Barnaby said, sounding steelier than usual.

"We need to talk. About Victor."

"I really don't want to have anything to do with him anymore. Or you."

"That's not your choice. You're still a potential co-conspirator."

"I told you what I knew."

"It's what you don't know that I'm interested in. I need you to get even palsier with him than before."

"Look, I'm just a time-and-motion man. That's all he needs me for, and he has a limited need."

"Offer to do some other businesses. I'm guessing he has them. That's what I need to know."

Barnaby thought about Victor's offer of a possible partnership but didn't share that with Zoot. Instead, he said, in a taunting tone: "I know two he doesn't have any more. I was there when the bad news came in."

Zoot smiled.

"If those are his businesses, I need proof. His manager denies Victor's the owner. I need books, letters, or maybe you can draw him out. Use your recorder again. Or even better...."

"No, please. Whatever it is. Not me."

"This'll work, and I know you can do it."

Barnaby sighed.

"What?"

"Plant one more bug. In his office at the fish factory."

*　　*　　*

Barnaby called on Monday to set up an appointment with Victor to talk about future business. He didn't think Victor would be that interested in chatting after what had happened to the factory and the computer operation. But to Barnaby's surprise, Victor agreed immediately to a meeting. He seemed unusually eager.

That Wednesday, Barnaby sat down at Victor's Hunts Point fish office to make his pitch to examine any other business that might need help. But Victor wasn't interested in talking about that. It became pretty evident right away that he'd had Barnaby come by for quite another reason.

"Remember that little pistol I gave you to protect yourself against the Chinese guys?" he said.

Barnaby's throat constricted at the words, and he just nodded, happy that he hadn't had a chance to plant Zoot's bug, which he'd left in his car.

"I had a kind of funny report from a little birdie down at the New York Police Department. Seems the cops in your village, who aren't really equipped to do much in the way of forensics, sent a bullet from a local home invasion-murder in your neck of the woods. Turns out, the bullet in question came from that gun."

"I thought you said it was untraceable."

"Not traceable to me, yes. It belonged to an ex-pal of mine who is no longer with us after using it in sort of a sloppy way. It was traceable to him."

"I see."

"So I'm wondering how that happened. You haven't been a bad boy, have you, Barnaby?"

"I threw that gun away. I didn't want to tell you because it would have seemed ungrateful."

"Oh, that's a good story. I like that story. I might have used it myself in a similar situation, but you know the problem with that story?"

Barnaby shook his head.

"It seems you knew the victim. Pretty well, in fact."

"I'm not sure what you mean."

"Oh, I think you do. Barbara was her name. Barbara Wade. Ring a bell?"

Barnaby nodded his head.

"Look, I'm not the cops," Victor said, "so you don't have to worry about me, and I take it the gun is disposed of, so what could I prove, other than I gave it to you out of friendship?"

"Uh-huh."

"But I wouldn't do that. Call the cops, I mean. It's the last thing in the world I would do, because we're business colleagues. Right?"

"Right."

Victor leaned back in his chair, waited a beat then asked: "So what did happen? Just between us."

"Uh," Barnaby said, at a loss for words.

"I hear she was terminally ill. That it?"

Barnaby formulated his answer and decided to take a chance. Even though he'd had no experience in such matters, it seemed like the smart move.

"Yes."

"Wow. Double wow."

"She was my wife's best friend."

Victor let out a small snort of breath.

"You got more stones than I imagined."

Barnaby got a puzzled look on his face.

"You know, cojones. Balls."

"Ah, right. I guess I didn't think of it in that way."

"Whatever. The main thing is that you showed me I might be able to use a guy like you."

Barnaby nodded.

"I'll be happy to help if I can. You have another business you want me to look at?"

"I was actually thinking of something bigger. You have a great look about you. Nobody suspects you of anything. That can be useful to someone like me. I got other people, but they're sort of known, so I could really use someone new. Someone I can trust. Someone who's been straight with me. Someone I know some things about."

Barnaby realized what he was hearing was more a threat than a compliment.

"Down the road, we could be sorta partners. You could sign some contracts and the like." Victor sniffed inward as he pondered something. "But there is one thing I do need to get straight first."

"Sure."

"You visited a friend of mine recently. Er, not really a friend. More like an associate. Kristal. Kristal Power. That's her business name, anyway."

"Doesn't sound familiar."

"Lives in your town. Nice looking lady. Hennaed hair. Wears suits."

Barnaby considered saying she was just one of the people he followed because of his new hobby, but that might mean he'd have to explain about John Lin or Dora, so he just lied. But then his first lie led to another.

"I'm afraid there was a misunderstanding. She was offering something I didn't want."

"But why were you there?"

"Ah, I guess I was a little curious. I will say that."

"But in the end you backed off."

"Right. She's a little scary."

"But young girls aren't?"

Barnaby was puzzled.

"You don't mean Tesla, I hope."

"No, no. I'm talking Dora Pivo. It's come to my attention you took some rather naughty photos of her at an establishment I am familiar with."

Barnaby's eyes blinked as he tried to figure out how Victor would have known about the photos he'd given to Zoot. He decided it couldn't have come from that FBI. Victor must have somehow heard about it from her or someone she told. Her dad?

"She, uh, tricked me. She asked me to take those photos and then...."

Victor put up his hands, palms facing Barnaby.

"Hey, you don't have to explain to me. Seems like you got a healthy interest in the ladies, young and otherwise."

Barnaby decided to quit while he was ahead and said nothing.

Hearing no response, Victor said: "Glad that's settled, so let's get down to business."

"OK," Barnaby said, sounding a bit like a robot.

"Just as a reminder, then: My No. 1 rule, if we're gonna do some business together, is what?"

Barnaby searched his memory for what Victor had said about that. He remembered. "Loyalty," he said. As he gave the answer almost reflexively, he immediately remembered the double game Zoot wanted him to play with Victor. The very epitome of disloyalty. He quickly wiped that conflicting notion from his mind and said, in a bright tone: "I already follow that rule. It's a little like 'The customer is always right.'"

Victor grimaced a bit.

"Not exactly. If you break my rule, the consequences can be a lot more negative than losing my business."

After the meeting with Victor, Barnaby met Zoot back in the city as they had agreed. Zoot was angry that Barnaby hadn't planted the bug in Victor's office.

"There was no way. We talked in his office, then he showed me out. I had no time alone there."

"All right. But we'll have to think of something for your next visit. Maybe a distraction that makes him leave the office. Like a fire."

Barnaby searched for something to change the subject.

"There is some good news: He wants me to help on some things in the future. If I prove my loyalty."

"More businesses?"

"I don't know. He said something about signing contracts."

"A front man! That could be great. Why do you think he wants your help?"

"He said he thinks he can trust me."

* * *

Barnaby took the train home. He was daydreaming out the window on the river side and didn't pay as much attention to the passengers as he usually did on the ride in or back. He'd pretty much decided that his people-watching hobby wasn't really right for him. He'd decided to give it up and stick to what he knew.

The train pulled into his stop, and he walked mindlessly to the exit. After he got to the edge of the parking lot, he heard a young girl's voice behind him yell, "Hey, creep!"

He turned and saw it was Dora, dressed in form fitting blue jeans, a tight yellow sweater and a black leather jacket. She walked up to him, her eyes narrowed.

"Heard you were poking around my house."

"That's not true. I don't even know where you live."

"With my Auntie Kristal. You followed her home, she told me."

The penny dropped.

"Oh, yes. I didn't realize she was your aunt."

"I told you the last time not to go butting in where you're not wanted. It just leads to trouble, and I'm the expert on that."

Barnaby looked confused.

"You know what Dora stands for?"

"I didn't know it stood for anything."

"Pandora, which was my mother's stupid idea. She was reading Edith Fuckin' Hamilton's book on Greek myths when she was pregnant with me. You know it?"

"I, I never really went in for Greek stories much."

"That explains a lot. You would have known you don't go opening things up without knowing what's inside."

"I meant no harm."

"Too late. My dad's getting out of prison. And I told him all about you. The stalking and that photo you took of me."

"That was your idea!"

"Tell it to him. He said he was dying to meet you. Dying."

* * *

Dora walked off ahead of Barnaby. In a bit of a trance, he watched her shapely behind hypnotically twitch back and forth. He was in danger of going into a trance until a black blot in the air to his right distracted his attention. At first he thought it was a hawk. Then he got a better look at its head, as the ugly mug of a circling turkey vulture came into view, soaring on a thermal over the station in search of dinner. After about 30 seconds, the raptor began a dive, apparently having spotted something tasty in the area between the train station and the river.

Watching birds had always put Barnaby in mind of predator and prey, and most of the time he found himself rooting for the bird that found breakfast or dinner in the waters or on the land near his home. He tracked the survivors. In a friendly way, they were his prey, though he wished them no harm. But as the turkey vulture slipped behind the roof of the station, Barnaby silently mouthed a short prayer for whatever little creature was racing for cover, its heartbeat in panic mode as its sympathetic nervous system loosened its bladder and constricted its sphincter muscles.

Barnaby walked home and puttered around the house, checking out his refrigerator and cabinets without being able to settle on what to eat that night. He noticed on his pet charts that it was time to feed Hortense and Herpie, but he had no proper reptile food for them, having forgotten to stop at the pet store. It had been a very inefficient, disorganized day for a time-and-motion man.

He pored himself a glass of water from the kitchen tap and sat down at his laptop. He opened his browser, and on a whim again, searched for "Pandora." He was looking for something that might help. He wasn't quite sure why he thought it might be there. But there was something.

Victor and Zoot wanted pieces of him, and Dora's father appeared to be right behind in the threat line. Barnaby tried to think of a way out of his predicament, but other than somehow going back in time to the day before he began his people-watching hobby, he couldn't. The story of Pandora, which he discovered was about a jar, not a box as most people thought, did offer some hope. In fact, that is precisely what it was famous for offering.

Hope, the story went, was the only thing that remained in Pandora's mythic jar when she managed to put the lid back on after letting out all the evils of the world. Hoping for the best might not the smartest move, but Barnaby embraced it. It was all he had, so he got himself a pad of paper and pen and wrote out a to-do list for the next day in the expectation that he would still be alive to deal with it.

He put nothing about Tesla on his list, which comprised more mundane things like checking out who was running the caring committee, picking up food for Tesla's pets and taking the next steps to kickstart his new consulting business.

* * *

Barnaby, however, was on a list Tesla was compiling. Worried about the vibes she was picking up from him as he described his recent days, she'd asked Veronica to meet in the park again. The soccer players weren't there, but an informal game of American football was in progress as they watched from their usual bench.

Veronica, outfitted stylishly as always, had an ankle length turquoise belted trench coat, which she wore open, Matrix style. Underneath she had on a white broadcloth man's shirt and black jeans over cowboy boots with inlays of turquoise leather. Tesla just wore baggy jeans and an Irish sweater.

"Sounds like he's at that old rock-and-a-hardplace place," Veronica said after hearing the litany of threats against Barnaby.

"I'm worried what'll happen after I go off to school." Tesla smiled coyly. "Maybe I should just stay here and help him out."

Veronica's eye crinkled.

"Sounds like the beginning of negotiations. I help him or you can't go. That it?"

Tesla adopted a poker face.

"Maybe."

Veronica let out a small laugh.

"I thought I was supposed to be the one who was in charge in this relationship."

Tesla smiled.

"So will you help him, fearless leader?"

"Well, on Zoot, we have a little something on him. Bit of a nasty habit that he wouldn't want others to know about. And aside from his personal life, it seems he's been a little fast and loose when it comes to installing phone taps and electronic bugs. I don't think he'll want to have his boss learning about that. Maybe we can persuade him to transfer Barnaby to the agency as its confidential informant. As for Dora's dad, when he gets out, he'll be on parole, so he has to mind his manners. We'll probably be able to nail him on insider trading, building on some conversations we've become aware of. We can also let his parole officer know of his interest in Barnaby and warn him that if anything happens, he goes back in the slammer."

"And Victor?"

"Dragon is another matter. He's up to his eyeballs in Chinese deals we'd like to know more about. We shut down that one in the Garment District, and are expelling a couple of his pals, but they're like cockroaches. They'll pop up somewhere when the lights go out, so we need Barnaby – and maybe even you, cheerleading in the background."

"Any chance Victor will just wind up in prison for the counterfeit or computer stuff?"

Veronica shook her head.

"Looks like he's going to beat the rap. Seems Zoot Ames didn't do all the right paperwork on his bugs and wiretaps, so the incriminating stuff about Victor gets tossed. But Victor and the Chinese have a lot more things going than that little garment factory, so we're not too broken up about that. We'll get him and them eventually."

"And you're sure you can't do it without Barnaby?"

Veronica shook her head.

"He's made himself sort of indispensible."

Chapter 22

After Sadie Tucker took over the caring committee in the village, Barnaby helped her get ready for the Christmas deliveries. Thanksgiving had gone off without a hitch thanks to Barbara's advance planning. Barnaby had spent the holiday with Tesla and her mother. The mood had been mixed. Tesla was pumped about going off to school. Her mother was cautious about the big change in her daughter's life. Barnaby pretended to be happy as the drumsticks and butternut squash got passed around. But with his life in danger, inwardly his stomach was in knots and his mind was fretting, an anxiety that lasted past that day of feasting.

He'd made that chipper to-do list in a glimmer of hope after his encounter with Dora and her legendary namesake. Leaving his ill-chosen hobby in the dust, he'd written down some steps to get his new business on track. But Victor was the only real client he could claim. Every other owner had said he'd think about it. The optimistic list had sat on his kitchen counter unattended for days, a victim of coffee stains and a lack of interest. He'd decided pursuing a business while people might want to hurt or even kill him wasn't realistic, and eventually he'd torn up the list.

Victor was drawing ever closer, trying to use Barnaby's legitimacy to finance new operations. Zoot kept pushing to get a bug planted in Victor's fish warehouse office, and he got angrier every time Barnaby said he hadn't been able to do it because there were too many people around. The truth was, Barnaby just didn't want to do it.

A black man in the snakeskin boots came by and said he'd soon be taking over from Zoot, probably after the first of the year. With a new devil replacing the old one, quite a different plan formed in Barnaby's head as the walls of his life closed in. There was still some hope in it, but it was more realistic.

He gathered some reference materials ranging from self-help Spanish books to Paul Theroux's "The Old Patagonia Express." He bought a new compact camera with a bigger sensor and a bottle of Imodium. He dug out his passport from his safe-deposit box.

He arranged to have his bills paid automatically by his bank, which did direct deposits of his paychecks. He had two years of salary coming, his house was paid off, and he had a tidy sum in savings beyond his pension and 401(k) money. If he didn't go crazy on the spending side, he didn't really have to start a new business. He could survive financially. But he needed a way to survive physically. And by the week before Christmas, he thought he'd worked out how to do that.

On Christmas Day Tesla came over with her gift.

"It's used, but it's in great shape," she explained, handing over a wrapped iPad. "I got it on eBay. It's just a Wi-Fi version, but that's all you really need."

"It's wonderful!"

"I put all your bird stuff on there, so you can take it to the point or wherever if you need to look something up. Got all the bird calls on it, too."

"You really shouldn't have," Barnaby said, turning the tablet on. "I know money can be tight at home."

"I came into some money, a little bonus, so it wasn't so hard."

Barnaby clicked on a couple of icons on the screen and played with the device for a moment. He put the gift down and walked over to his small, reusable metal Christmas tree to get another gift. It was in a long box wrapped in green foil paper with a scarlet, felt ribbon. Tesla opened it carefully, but it didn't take long for her to see what it was from the picture on the box.

"A bow!"

"Olympic-issue."

"This is fab, Mr. G," she said as she tore the rest of the paper off the box and opened it."

"You can practice a little in the backyard till you get a proper target range. I hired a service to come buy and check the house periodically if there's a freeze or windstorm or something. I'll have a timer on some of the lights, but you have your key. Come over whenever you want. And speaking of keys, I have a little used gift for you too."

Barnaby handed over the keys to his Honda and an envelope with the title and registration made over to Tesla.

"Your car?"

"I won't be needing one for a while, and I never did use it very much. I figured you'd need some way to get your menagerie out to California. After that movie, people aren't too keen about snakes on a plane."

"Are you going somewhere?"

Barnaby nodded.

"I need a little change of scenery -- and distance between me and some people.

"I think I know who...Where you going?"

"I'll let you know. I'm buying some time to see how it goes."

"What if somebody wants to come after you?"

"I'm hoping I'll be far enough away to make it inconvenient. I'm not a fugitive or anything, and other than leaving a record of crossing a border, no one will really know where I am at any given time."

"How about me?"

"Well, now that I have my iPad, we can talk by e-mail."

"We should use some new e-mail addresses. I'll set some up."

Barnaby nodded at the idea.

"Make mine HudsonHawk."

* * * * *

Barnaby planned his escape with the same meticulous detail he'd exhibited with time-and-motion clients of Montgomery & Co. He withdrew modest amounts from his bank account each day until he had just under $10,000, a sum he wouldn't have to declare when he crossed the border.

He laid out a backpack and the sort of items he might carry if he were going out for a birding event: binoculars, his new camera, a coffee thermos, a waterproof windbreaker and matching waterproof pants, a compass, walking shoes, jeans, a cotton sweater, a baseball cap with a long bill and a portable radio.

He also purchased some bird guides and train route maps. To avoid any questions about where he might be headed, he arranged a mailbox at a UPS store in Laredo, which is where he planned to leave the country. He mailed the guides and maps to himself.

Among his train books, he had a huge one on Grand Central, and he studied the floor plans of the vast terminal to plot a very specific escape route. He liked the idea that the author of "The Old Patagonia Express" had for beginning his train odyssey: a ride on a subway line.

The day of his departure, Barnaby took the same commuter train he had for years to Montgomery & Co., but instead of his usual car, he walked to the south end of the platform and got into the front of the train so he'd be among the first into the terminal. He wanted to avoid any of the regulars, especially Dora or Kristal. In keeping with his charade, he had his binoculars looped around his neck and had a book on the birds of Central Park on his lap.

When he got to Grand Central, he hotfooted it to an elevator he'd located a floor plan of his terminal book. Normally the elevators were used by elderly or fat people who didn't want to deal with stairs or escalators. They were in out-of-the- way places, and most commuters never noticed them.

When he approached the one he'd chosen, only an older woman with a walker was waiting inside. The doors began to close. Barnaby shoved his knapsack between them to keep them open. He got into the car and noticed a familiar heavy-set man jogging toward the car from about 50 yards away. He put up the index finger of his right hand as if he planned to hold the car. But he leaned over to the control panel and pushed the "Close Doors" button firmly. The doors shut, leaving Crunch about 20 yards short of his goal.

The elevator went down and let Barnaby out, as he had planned, some distance from the closest stairs, the only way for Crunch or anyone to catch up with him. Normally he would have given the woman the courtesy of letting her get out first, but given the situation, he bolted from the elevator and headed down an unoccupied track on the edge of the lower level. He stationed himself behind a pillar to hide from any interested parties. He took out his guide to Central Park birds and read it for a couple of minutes in case someone like Crunch found him and asked what the was doing. No one did, and after a few moments, he peered around the pillar and found the coast was clear.

He scooted southeast across the terminal and headed for the subway lines below Grand Central. He took the shuttle to Times Square, positioning himself in the first car again to make sure he was ahead of the exiting crowd. He felt almost smug about his escape routine at that moment, but he didn't notice that Crunch had just made it into the last car of the train.

After getting to Times Square, Barnaby made it to Penn Station and headed for one of the main men's rooms. He went into a stall and took off his light parka and put on a ratty old sweater that he'd found in his closet. He jammed a knit hat over his ears and put his backpack in a large black garbage bag.

Crunch came into the men's room looking for Barnaby. The place was full of homeless men, stripped to the waist and soapy, taking advantage of the free hot water in the sinks in the facility. Not seeing Barnaby, Crunch stationed himself at the entrance so he could watch the rest room and the main waiting area for his prey.

Barnaby waited for a couple of the homeless men to get dressed and march out of the men's room on their way to panhandle arriving commuters. In his disguise, he looked so much like them that he passed by Crunch without the muscle man noticing. In one of the only benefits of his ill-advised hobby, Barnaby had used the tradecraft he'd developed in following commuters to get out of town without any of his adversaries being able to stop him.

* * * * *

After Barnaby disappeared in early January, Tesla came over to his house regularly to feed her pets or to watch a movie or the Jets on his big-screen TV. In the those early days, Tesla found Barnaby was receiving voice-mail messages from Zoot and Victor, who'd somehow been told Barnaby was out of town dealing with a death in the family.

Zoot sounded angry that Barnaby wasn't returning his calls. One Sunday in mid-January, he knocked on Barnaby's door and pressed the buzzer a couple of times. Tesla answered, wearing Hortense around her neck.

Zoot looked surprised at Tesla and her snake.

"Where's Barnaby?"

"Don't know?"

"When'll he be back?"

"No idea."

"His car's out front."

"Yep."

"So he couldn't have gone far."

"I guess."

Zoot opened his briefcase, took out a business card and tried to hand it to Tesla.

"Call me if you see him, would you?"

Tesla had both hands busy with Hortense and said, "I'll just have him call you if I hear from him."

Zoot tossed the card back in his case on top of the transcript he'd just gotten from the wiretap at Madam Selma's. He closed the case and thought a moment about whether to ask the question that was suddenly in his mind.

"One other thing," he asked.

"Yeah?"

"You don't happen to know where Dora Pivo lives, do you?"

Tesla told him, and Zoot headed there. It was mid-afternoon. There was a light dusting of snow on the lawn of Kristal's stucco house. He parked in front of her Infiniti and went up the front walk.

There was no bell so he used the metal knocker, which was in the form of a fist. Kristal answered the door, a glass of wine in hand. She was dressed in tight black jeans and a bulky black sweater. Her feet were bare. Her toenails were painted blood red.

"Yes?" she asked in a bored tone, taking a sip of wine.

Normally Zoot would have identified himself as an FBI agent because of the leverage his credentials gave him in almost any situation, but he found himself saying instead: "Is Dora home?" as if he wanted her to come out and play.

"What do you want with her?"

"I just need to talk to her."

"That's what the last guy said. Cost him $500."

* * * * *

Zoot didn't get to see Dora that day. Kristal said if it turned out Dora wasn't what he was really looking for, he should come back and maybe they could work something out. If Zoot had come by a few days earlier, he might have seen Barnaby behind some tall bushes across the street, using a long-lens to take a photo of Kristal as she left for work on her bike. And if Zoot could have had access to a high-resolution spy satellite — the kind that lets the NSA read the lettering on a pack of cigarettes all the way from space — he might have spied one Barnaby Gilbert, train and bird aficionado. Barnaby was sitting in a window seat looking at that very image of Kristal on his used iPad as his train, en route from Cuzco to Puno, passed three squat women in derby hats tending alpacas at 14,000 feet in the Andes. In his mouth was Mr. Bannister's contraband Cohiba, lit and being enjoyed. It was a moment of respite in what Barnaby hoped would be the beginning of a smart move.

Afterword

If you are familiar with birding or the criminal cases to be found in New York City's courts, you probably recognized some of the people and plot elements of "The Commuter." Wildlife along the Hudson River is abundant, as I found out the day I moved to the village just north of Barnaby Gilbert's fictive home and spotted my first bald eagle in flight over the train station. In my work as a journalist I also encountered some not so rare examples of the human species, from Eastern European hackers who prey on people's bank accounts to Chinese industrial spies who are more likely to steal your company's trade secrets or intellectual property.

Purveyors of counterfeit goods can be found most famously near New York's Canal Street, where a character like Jasmine or her hidden closet of fake, unassembled designer bags would not seem fanciful to local denizens or veteran tourists.

It might seem that the people Barnaby Gilbert encountered in his dangerous hobby are a bit over-the-top, even for a work of fiction. But you don't have to scratch hard in a city that supposedly has 8 million stories to find it teeming with the sort of players in Barnaby's tale. Their saga starts with the what-if question of a commuter suddenly set free to indulge a longtime fantasy. Your own results might not be so different in the real world should you dare to give it a try, but please don't tell anyone I suggested the idea. In my world, I try to avoid Greek tragedy and only open Pandora's jar in the pages of a book.

Acknowledgments

Most novelists get help in shaping and publishing a book, and I've had plenty. Fellow editors and reporters at Bloomberg News and members of my local book club were guinea pigs for initial drafts of The Commuter and other works in progress.

At Bloomberg, they include: Jeff Burke, Charles Carter, Andrew Dunn, Mary Romano, Dave Rovella and Linda Sandler. My Croton-on-Hudson book crew includes: Les Andrews, Chuck and Heather Cooper, Jeff Kellgren and Loomis Mayer.

My agent Bob Thixton of the Pinder Lane agency has read and advised on multiple versions of my books. He knows what works and what doesn't and was encouraging in early days when I need the encouragement.

A special thanks to Norm Pearlstine for introducing me to Bob.

I thank my son Alex, a millennial, for unwittingly giving me story ideas picked up from listening to him and his friends, and my wife Sally for putting up with my typing on weekends and vacations, when we could have been outdoors getting some exercise or having fun.

Made in the USA
San Bernardino, CA
21 July 2014